I'm Not the Only Murderer in my Retirement Home

Also by Fergus Craig

Once Upon a Crime
Murder at Crime Manor

I'm Not the Only Murderer in my Retirement Home

FERGUS CRAIG

SPHERE

SPHERE

First published in Great Britain in 2026 by Sphere

1 3 5 7 9 10 8 6 4 2

Copyright © Fergus Craig 2026

The moral right of the author has been asserted.

All characters and events in this publication, other than those clearly in the public domain, are fictitious and any resemblance to real persons, living or dead, is purely coincidental.

All rights reserved.
No part of this publication may be reproduced, stored in a retrieval system, or transmitted, in any form, or by any means, without the prior permission in writing of the publisher, nor be otherwise circulated in any form of binding or cover other than that in which it is published and without a similar condition including this condition being imposed on the subsequent purchaser.

A CIP catalogue record for this book is available from the British Library.

Hardback ISBN 978-1-4087-3462-9
Trade paperback ISBN 978-1-4087-2482-8

Typeset in Bembo by M Rules
Printed and bound in Great Britain by Clays Ltd

Papers used by Sphere are from well-managed forests and other responsible sources.

Sphere
An imprint of
Little, Brown Book Group
Carmelite House
50 Victoria Embankment
London EC4Y 0DZ

The authorised representative
in the EEA is
Hachette Ireland
8 Castlecourt Centre
Dublin 15, D15 XTP3, Ireland
(email: info@hbgi.ie)

An Hachette UK Company
www.hachette.co.uk

www.littlebrown.co.uk

To my mum, who taught me to read.

ONE

Seven was Carol's number. Not a big number. Pathetic really, stopped before she got started, but it was enough to call her a serial killer. Enough to make her point.

Or was it more? Convicted for seven anyway. Perhaps there were a few others – it all got a bit hazy towards the end there. Harold Shipman had got through hundreds, but that was easy. A doctor killing patients, old ladies who walked into his surgery. They were sitting ducks, hardly worth the effort. Tap-ins. Now, picking seven (or whatever her number was) moving targets, young healthy people, going about their business, and *murdering* them, that took skill. That took guts.

Of course, this was all in the past. Now Carol could hardly be bothered to get up and find the TV remote, let alone chase down a man, knock him to the ground, stab him in the neck, drag him into the van, take him for a drive, bury him in the woods, clean up and leave a clue for the police to make it interesting. Carol was retired now. Which was why she was heading to Sheldon Oaks to be with the rest of the retirees, the rest of the sitting ducks.

Want to know how to knock a few decades off your sentence? Tell them where the bodies are buried. Carol's choice was a popular one – Epping Forest. The only problem was finding a patch of ground without a body already in it. You'd think the difficulty would be getting the corpse out of the van and dragging it deep enough into the woods, but things were different back then. After dark, there'd always be someone else with their own body to ditch. Usually, the other killer would be a professional, a gangster, something like that – not a simple hobbyist like Carol. You'd help them to carry theirs, they'd help you with yours – a real sense of community. People were friendlier in the old days, not like it is now.

Carol noticed the sound of tyres on gravel, a noise she hadn't heard in years, as the taxi slowly pulled into the driveway. She braced herself for a new beginning, her new placid existence. The driver, who hadn't said a word on the journey, took her luggage from the boot as Carol looked at her new home. The frontage was big and rectangular. Carol hadn't a clue of the history but to her it looked like a converted grand hotel, at least a hundred years old. Downton Abbey, but every character is Maggie Smith's age. Sheldon Oaks was in Hampstead, a wealthy part of North London; its pretty grounds bordering Hampstead Heath. This was the sort of place the rich came to die.

Carol walked into the plush lobby area.

'Oh dear. Ms Quinn. Welcome. I'm terribly sorry but I don't think your removals people have arrived.' Elisa, the concierge, had dark hair, expensive glasses, and was well put-together but currently fretting. She spoke in a European accent. Everything here had class, thought Carol, like a five-star hotel that only accepted guests over the age of sixty-five. Elisa walked over to her from behind the reception desk.

'That's all right. I didn't use a removals service,' said Carol.

'Oh, I see. You have some family helping you? Are they here? Let me get you a seat.'

Carol remained standing. 'No. Just me. I have this but that will be all.' She nodded down to her wheelie case, small enough to qualify as hand luggage for the overhead locker on most flights.

'So the rest of your things will be arriving another day?'

'No, no. This is it. Thank you. If my apartment is ready, I'd like to move in, please.'

Elisa failed to disguise her shock. This was not a normal arrival, clearly. Most new residents, Carol supposed, came to Sheldon Oaks having gone through months of packing, organising possessions accumulated over a lifetime. Many arrived traumatised, no doubt, after taking the contents of a four-floor house and downsizing enough to fit them into a one-room apartment, their adult children standing over them, lecturing them about how this was for the best, assuring them that the urgency with which they were moving them into a home had absolutely nothing to do with a desire to sell the family's biggest asset at the top of the housing market.

Here was Carol Quinn, seventy-five, short and scrappy, with shoulder-length grey hair and a small visor cap, arriving in a cab straight from prison.

'Ms Quinn!' Giles Temple, the owner, emerged from a back room. 'Let me take that for you. Journey okay?'

'Yes, thank you.'

Carol recognised Giles from the brochures. In photographs he'd been smartly suited and airbrushed. In person, you got a sense of who the real Giles Temple was. Fortyish and out of shape, with blue eyes and chaotic blond hair, wearing an old-fashioned hooped rugby shirt and tattered aqua blue shorts. It was the sort of outfit that only a man with an expensive education could get away with.

Giles lowered his voice. 'And did you come straight from . . .?'

'Prison, yes.'

'Surrey. That's right, Surrey,' said Giles, placing a glossier spin on her answer.

Carol was aware that Giles and Elisa had had discussions about the ethics of welcoming a recent lag, a convicted serial killer no less, into their luxury retirement community directly from HMP Bronzefield. When making arrangements, they'd accidentally forwarded Carol their whole email conversation on the subject and were still apparently unaware that she had read it all. Giles and Elisa had agreed there was a balance to be struck. Yes, with this particular resident there was a higher than comfortable possibility of her murdering a significant percentage of the Sheldon Oaks 'family', but on the other hand, in this day and age, did they really have the right to be so prejudiced? Carol was being released for a reason. She was reformed, wasn't she? They had to have faith in the criminal justice system. Who were they to judge another human being who'd paid their debt to society? Also, new purchases had been far lower than projected in recent months, the accounts weren't looking great, and Carol had offered not to rent but to buy an apartment outright, at full price and in cash. If that meant there was the ever-so-slight risk of them all being slaughtered one by one – blood seeping from the cracks in the windows, trickling down into Hampstead, drowning the city in gore – it was a risk they were prepared to take.

With Elisa and Giles gone, Carol sat on a wicker chair on her new balcony, enjoying the early-summer sunshine. A few weeks ago, she'd been allowed out for the day to tour her new apartment. Floor-to-ceiling windows, hardwood floors. The last time she'd had her own place everyone wanted carpet.

Her kitchen intimidated her. It had one of those ovens you see on cookery shows where the door disappears underneath when you open it, and a fridge with a thing in the door that you could push a glass into and ice would pop out. The TV was six times bigger than any she'd ever owned. Most decadent of all, her bedroom was en-suite, which meant she had *two* bathrooms. Her bladder wasn't as strong as it used to be, granted, but even at her age she had need for only one bathroom at any one time.

The brochure described the 'design ethic' as 'contemporary'. Carol, when telling her fellow inmates about it, opted for the word 'lovely'.

She had known for a while now that her lifestyle was about to change dramatically but it hadn't felt real until now. To actually be here, a free woman, living in the most luxurious surroundings, a world away from where she'd just spent hour after hour, day after day, year after year. *Thirty-five years.* Carol had earned this.

She looked out over the pretty gardens and sighed in satisfaction. No high walls, no barbed wire, no screws. No nerks in jogging bottoms using their one hour outdoors to drag pensively on a cigarette and tell, for the eight-hundredth time, the story of how 'everything went wrong when I met Darren'. Just some flowerbeds and a freshly cut lawn with a game of croquet in progress. A young man was banging in a post for a rope fence that marked the border between the lawns and the driveway. Everything was orderly here, everything was quaint. And beyond the grounds of Sheldon Oaks was Hampstead Heath, a paradise that overlooked her favourite city, a city she could now enjoy any time she liked.

Not now, though, because Carol had just remembered her bed. She walked through her one-floor flat and into her bedroom. There it was. Thirty-five years of sleeping on a paper-thin, less-than-single mattress, and now she was looking at a giant double bed. And it was all hers.

Carol kicked off her slip-ons, lay back and closed her eyes. She soon fell into a deep and peaceful sleep, dreaming of the last time she was in a bed this size, methodically cutting off a man's ear with a pair of nail scissors she'd bought that afternoon from Boots.

TWO

'You're making me nervous.'

This was at a time when the simple act of making Viennese Whirls could still put a resident on edge. Before the murders.

'Does it say that the tablespoon should be heaped? Because you've just put a heaped tablespoon in the bowl, and a heaped tablespoon is not a tablespoon. It's effectively a tablespoon and a half.'

'Does it really matter, Geoffrey?' said Margaret.

'I'm just saying . . .'

Here we go, thought Carol.

Geoffrey leant forward to emphasise the brilliance of his statement. 'I'm just saying baking is a *science,* not an art form.'

Geoffrey had said this many, many times before.

'I could strangle him, I really could,' Carol muttered to Margaret, under her breath. Margaret let out a quick little yelp of laughter, oblivious to the truth of Carol's statement.

'You're doing super, girls,' said Desmond, from his chair. 'Ignore Geoff. He's an arsehole.' Desmond's blue eyes twinkled with mischief.

'All I'm saying is that . . .'

'We all know what you're saying, Geoffrey,' said Margaret. 'Really, we do. *Thank you.*'

The group had been spending Friday mornings in the communal kitchen for six weeks or so. Elisa, the concierge, the lady who ran the day-to-day business of Sheldon Oaks, had put up a poster for 'Bake Off Fridays' and a few of the more active residents had signed up. There were a lot more activities on offer since Elisa had started working there, people said. She had an energy about her.

At first, they'd all mucked in together in the kitchen, but you could quickly see that that wasn't going to work. Too many cooks and all that. Carol and Margaret had ended up doing most of the baking. Sometimes Desmond would get a burst of enthusiasm, start mixing something, realise he was more of a hindrance than a help and return to his chair. Carol suspected that Catherine, who was currently reading on the sofa, had retreated from the actual baking because she didn't want to embarrass the others. In the first week, she'd effortlessly put together the most magnificent custard slices. Flaky, light, really – just to die for. Since then she'd stepped back. Perhaps she'd looked at the disasters the others were plating up and felt like an adult joining in an under-tens football match.

So Carol and Margaret were the only remaining actual bakers, but the group was the group and here they gathered every Friday at 10.30 a.m.

Light, dappled by the summer leaves, shone in from a courtyard and onto the marble countertops. At the edge, away from the kitchen island, there were a sofa and a couple of sleek armchairs. Kitchens, for Carol, had been functional rooms, where work got done. This was foreign to her: a kitchen built purely for leisure. She liked it.

Elisa popped her head in. 'Everything okay, ladies?' She nodded at the men. 'Gentlemen.'

Carol still couldn't place Elisa's accent (possibly Spanish?) and had not yet asked her where she came from for fear of offending her. She'd heard something on the radio about how asking people where they came from was apparently a no-no now. She wasn't sure why. Some friendly curiosity was a good thing, wasn't it? Wasn't that how you got to know people? Surely if you meant well that was all that mattered. It wasn't like Carol was going to say, 'Where are you from?' and then Elisa would say, 'Madrid,' and then Carol would punch her in the face, spit on her, kick her to the ground. Carol would just say, 'Oh, you must miss the weather,' and then that would be a nice icebreaker to get the conversation rolling. Better not risk it, though. Carol wouldn't want to hurt her feelings. She'd always found navigating social niceties tricky. Perhaps that's what had led her in the direction of recreational murder.

'All good, thank you, Elisa,' said Carol.

'Lovely. Whatever you're making, save some for me.'

'I really wouldn't get your hopes up,' said Margaret. 'I'm not sure we've produced anything edible for weeks.'

'You ladies make me laugh,' said Elisa, as she left.

Carol had surprised herself with how quickly she'd slotted into Sheldon Oaks life. She supposed that, for all its comforts, all she'd really done was swap one institution for another. Yes, there was freedom here, yes, she was no longer surrounded by criminals, but there were plenty of similarities. This was a place that ran on routine. You saw the same faces every day. Most people ate the same food, had the same conversations.

And then there were the differences. Carol looked around her, as she often did now, and thought about all the killing implements that were suddenly available to her. Decades of not being trusted with metal cutlery and now, right in front of her, there was a knife rack. She could slice the arteries of everyone in this room in a minute. On the counter was a blender she could shove Margaret's hand into and turn it the colour of a chunky tomato soup. A mortar and pestle. Which was the mortar and which was the pestle? She wasn't sure, but she did know that either, with a force she was still capable of, could cave in a skull.

There was a sad irony to it. She'd given up killing for good and here she was, living in a murderer's paradise. Like a recovering alcoholic getting a job at an off-licence. She trusted herself not to relapse. These people were her friends and that impulse had left her. It belonged to the last century – but, oh, what a younger Carol Quinn could have done in this playground.

Desmond made a noise, using his stick to propel his sturdy frame into a standing position. 'I keep nodding off,' he said. 'Think I'll go for a lie-down. Got a busy afternoon planned.'

'Oh, yes?' said Margaret.

Desmond tapped his nose playfully. He liked to give the impression that he had a lot going on but Carol sensed that he didn't. A 'busy afternoon' probably meant the cricket was on TV.

'All right, Desmond,' said Margaret. 'We'll bring you a couple of biscuits if there are any.'

'I have faith in you all. Can I lick the bowl?'

Carol handed him a spoon, smiling.

'Delicious,' he said. 'Absolutely delicious.'

Once the whirls were in the oven, Margaret took Desmond's vacated seat and Carol hovered anxiously by the oven, checking the time twice a minute. Geoffrey tried to strike up a conversation about something in the news that day but nobody bit. They'd all learnt a while ago that he was just looking for an opportunity to show off. Geoffrey was the sort of man who started a lot of sentences with 'See, what you have to understand is . . .' There was no subject he was not prepared to monologue on for the benefit of the group. Arable farming, EU fishing quotas, a healthy diet, drill music, the Geneva Convention, vacuum-cleaner technology, the novels of Jilly Cooper (although he admitted to never having read one), stand-up comedy, the future of AI (which he insisted he understood but didn't have time to explain), climate change, the Japanese economy, the correct road to take to get to absolutely anywhere. Geoffrey was an expert on them all. A nice enough man, thought Carol, but not the sort of person you'd want to be stuck in a cell with. Unlikely anyway, seeing as he'd proudly announced within thirty seconds of meeting her that he was an ex-policeman. Not that that, in and of itself, bothered her particularly. Her gripe had never been with the police: it had been with her victims, the ones who had to die.

But this was pleasant. These were smart people, *nice* people. These were the sort of people Carol was happy to spend the rest of her days with. They didn't need to know about her past. What good would that do? Yes, Carol had been a killer but why should that define her? Some people were so obsessed with identity, these days. Carol would see it on social-media profiles, people reducing themselves to three or four labels: 'vegan, dentist, keen cyclist'; 'Welsh, socialist, Manchester United'.

The trouble was, as soon as you told someone you were once a serial killer, it was all they could think about. It was crazy! They could never seem to get past it. Carol would be standing there talking about how she used to like pork but now she found it too fatty or how there never seemed to be anything on the TV any more or how she'd heard that Americans don't call Lego 'Lego' but 'Legos' and she could tell that whoever she was speaking with was just thinking about her murders.

So, if no one else mentioned it, then neither would she. She'd told people in the home that she'd been a secretary and never married. Both were true. No one asked many further questions and Carol was happy that way.

'Carol, why don't you sit down?' said Catherine. 'All that fretting isn't going to help. They'll either bake properly or they won't. Geoffrey, be a gentleman and budge up for Carol.'

'Really, I'm fine,' said Carol.

'Oh, sorry, Carol. My head's in this bloody newspaper reading about this bloody government. Did you know—'

'Yes, I'm sure we all know, Geoffrey,' said Margaret. 'Now budge up for the lady.'

'Sorry. Sorry.' Geoffrey moved along the small two-seater sofa.

Well, Carol had to sit down now, seeing as such a palaver had been made of the whole thing. She took her place beside Geoffrey, with him, in that way that certain men do, spreading his legs wide, oblivious to the fact that this meant Carol had to make herself as small as she could.

'Sorry, Carol,' said Geoffrey. 'Take a load off.'

Carol and Geoffrey hadn't really spoken much one to one. Had Carol – now she had really to think here – had Carol sat this close to a man in thirty-five years? How absurd. Oh, yes, that God-awful moment when her mother died and the prison vicar had sat beside her on her bed and tried to comfort her when all she could think about was his coffee breath and how, in her younger days, that would have been enough for her to put him on her kill list.

Carol and Geoffrey caught each other's eye for a brief moment, each assessing the other. Oh, God, he wasn't one of those residents looking for romance, was he? Carol would see them sometimes, pairing off in the bar, slyly heading up to each other's apartments. Just hideous, the thought of it. Sex was, as far as Carol was concerned, like skateboarding – meant for younger bodies.

Geoffrey took off his reading glasses and looked at her.

'Carol, what's your surname?'

Was this his attempt at a chat-up line? Showing an interest in something other than his own vast intellect? 'Quinn.'

'Quinn?'

'That's my name.'

Geoffrey put his glasses back on and looked down at his newspaper, frowning, not reading. Carol realised that her time as just another resident was coming to an end.

'Huh. Quinn,' Geoffrey mumbled to himself.

Just then, Margaret jumped up, as much as it was possible for a woman in her late seventies to jump up. 'The whirls!'

'Oh, fuck!' said Carol, smelling the burning and noting to herself that that was probably the first time she'd used the F-word in this company. Oh, well. Keeping up appearances could only last so long.

THREE

Geoffrey opened the front door to his apartment. He'd spent the last half-hour tidying up, adding any stray newspapers to the pile on his bedroom floor, rinsing out his microwave meal trays and sticking them in the recycling bin. He'd looked at the bellows hanging on a hook on his living-room wall and thought about taking them down. Would that be considered eccentric? A pair of bellows but no fireplace? You've got to have something on your wall, though, haven't you? They'd been on the wall in his old house for years and he'd transferred them here without really thinking about it.

'Can I get you a drink? Sorry, I mean, hello, Margaret. Can I get you a drink?'

'Cup of tea? If you're having one?'

'Should have thought to boil the kettle before you got here really, shouldn't I?' he said, heading to the kitchen.

Geoffrey Standing was nervous. Other than his family, he'd never entertained guests at Sheldon Oaks. He knew he could be, as his wife Connie had described it, 'a bit much'. He knew without her by his side to rein him in and give him a nudge when he was getting out of hand that he could annoy people. Now that she'd been dead for five years, what was he to do? People don't change, not seventy-five years in anyway. Geoffrey just had an instinct, one he could never budge, to show off when he knew something. 'You want to educate everyone,' Connie would say. Geoffrey had never quite grasped why that was a bad thing and even though he understood that it wound people up, he couldn't stop. The neural pathways were set and neural pathways was exactly the sort of subject he enjoyed telling people about.

'Now. Margaret. I'm very much a bag-in-first man. Is that all right with you? Everything I've read on the subject says it's the right way to go.'

'Perfect. Thank you, Geoffrey.'

There was a knock at the door. Geoffrey peeped through the eyehole. 'It's Catherine,' he announced to Margaret, opening the door. 'Hello, Catherine. Can I get you a drink? Margaret and I are having tea. I've already made two cups but I've deliberately boiled enough water for three.'

Margaret watched Geoffrey floundering around, playing host, treating three cups of tea like a dinner party for twelve people. Didn't men get silly as they got older? Especially the ones who'd been married for fifty years and suddenly found themselves alone. Sad, really, but this was a time of life where they all found themselves confronted by stark realities. Geoffrey had the face of a man who'd never knowingly been in contact with moisturiser, his cheeks blotchy and red, though no more than most men of his age and skin-care regime. There were people who got thinner, smaller, as they aged, and there were people who widened.

Geoffrey was the latter. Big shoulders, forty-something inches of waist, and a white beard. He had all the right elements to make a Father Christmas but somehow didn't look anything like him.

With Margaret, at first, you noticed her clothes: blazers with shoulder pads, chunky pearl necklaces, tartan skirts. She wore her hair in a dyed black bob. In recent years she'd developed a waddle, thanks to her hips. She'd caught a glimpse of her gait in the window of John Lewis once and was so disgusted that she now did everything she could not to see it. She'd spent a lifetime hiding her gummy smile and now she had a waddle to worry about.

Margaret marvelled at Catherine. Everything she did had elegance. Tall and slim, with a long neck and the upright posture of a dancer fifty years her junior. She couldn't put a finger on why but Margaret always thought there was something Scandinavian about the way Catherine carried herself. Had Margaret the confidence to do so, she'd ask Catherine where she bought her clothes. Smart but not too smart, bold colours, lovely cuts. Trousers, not skirts. Cashmere sweaters, button-down blouses. The outfit always topped off with the perfect brooch. Never formal but never anything less than impressive. Catherine was effortless. Margaret had felt the same way about a girl at school sixty-something years ago. She just wanted to know what it would feel like to be her for a day. Though now Margaret was old enough and wise enough to understand that everyone had their own problems.

Once they were all sitting down and enough niceties had been said by all, Margaret, never one to fail to get to the point, did just that.

'Geoffrey, why did you invite us over? I got the impression you had some news.'

'Well, well, well. Now,' Geoffrey cleared his throat and adopted the demeanour of a man chairing a board meeting. 'Carol.'

'Carol, yes?' said Margaret.

For one awful moment Margaret thought that Geoffrey was about to reveal that Carol and he were dating and that this was his way of letting them both down lightly on the news that they were out of the running to be his lover.

'Carol Quinn,' said Geoffrey. 'That name mean anything to either of you?'

'I presume we're talking about Carol from baking?' said Catherine.

'Yes. Carol from baking. Margaret? *Quinn. Carol Quinn.* You remember Carol Quinn?'

'*No!*' Margaret put down her cup of tea, afraid that she might be about to lose control of her body.

Geoffrey nodded solemnly. 'I've been on the broadband internet on my desktop computer to refresh my memory. It's her.'

'This can't be true. I don't understand how.' Margaret searched her cup for more tea, finding only the bag.

'Can somebody tell me what's happening, please?' said Catherine.

'Geoffrey, were you on the force when . . . ?' asked Margaret.

'Part of the team who caught her. And I'm presuming her case crossed your desk . . .' said Geoffrey.

'I was home secretary. Did everything I could to pressure the courts into a life sentence. Thought I'd done as much.

Remember giving a statement about how she wouldn't be out for a very long time indeed. Not until the 2020s. And, well, I suppose . . . here we are. Dear God.'

Catherine raised her voice. 'Please . . . what on earth are you both talking about?'

Margaret turned to Catherine. 'Carol from baking is a convicted serial killer.'

FOUR

Carol had taken to carrying around poison. Just a little packet of strychnine, a white powder that at a glance looked like any other white powder. She'd had it in her handbag for about a month now after doing a week as a temp receptionist in a laboratory. She'd flirtatiously extracted some information from a young scientist in the canteen one day, then stayed late and made herself a little sample. Just the one packet. Enough to do the job, apparently, though there was many a time when she wished she'd stocked up. Would have made things a lot easier.

This was a long time ago, at the end of the seventies. Documentaries would have you believe that Britain was wall-to-wall punks and industrial strife but Carol didn't remember it that way. If she tried to picture the late seventies now, the biggest cultural change came not from the Sex Pistols or the emergence of Margaret Thatcher but from the microwave and the SodaStream. People's minds weren't on economic decline and the end of an empire. They were on the wonder of homemade fizzy pop.

People, back then, had started to annoy Carol, men particularly. Loudmouths on trains, gropey bosses, taxi drivers who farted as if they weren't sharing an enclosed space with another human being.

The poison was a comfort. Did she think she'd ever use it? Probably not. But the knowledge that she now had it within her power to take matters into her own hands added a thrill to the daily grind.

It was in the Red Lion on Walworth Road, on a Friday night in November, that Carol had begun her new pastime.

Television was so boring back then. Just a couple of channels. She liked to read but if it was a Friday and she had nothing else on, Carol liked to pop down to the Red Lion for a couple of Bacardi and Cokes. This was before the Sunday roastification of the London pub scene, when they were still all smoke-filled drinking dens with sticky carpets and an air of glamorous menace. Why might a man go to the pub on his own? For a bit of atmosphere, a couple of drinks in company, some music, maybe a game of pool? All the same reasons that Carol was there, yet some in the Red Lion could not get past the idea that she must, *simply must*, be a slut on the prowl.

Karl Chilvers was the worst. 'You all right, darling? Let me get you a drink, darling. Don't look at me like that, darling. I'm only touching your arse, darling.' The way he looked at her, *through* her, as if she were nothing but a means to an end, a gift that came with the pub to be leched over, to be claimed as a prize for the lucky winner, taken home and made use of.

So why did she still go there, if that was her experience? Because it was her *right*. She had had a hard week too. This was a *public* house and the fact that she possessed a womb did not disqualify her from enjoying what it had to offer.

It was at the pool table that Carol decided to murder Karl Chilvers. She was good at pool. She was about to beat him for the third time in a row but that hadn't stopped him telling her how to play each shot, pointing to exactly where she ought to hit the object ball, even putting his arms around her, 'teaching' her how to hold a cue.

She watched him assess the table. Thought of how she'd seen him shout at his daughter in the street back in spring, how his girlfriend Denise had had a black eye last week, of how grating his loud, not-an-ounce-of-self-doubt South London voice was.

Leave the world a better place than when you got there. By ridding it of Karl Chilvers, she'd be working towards that.

On the back of the chair she was sitting on hung his leather bomber jacket. She put her hand into its right pocket.

No.

Then its left.

Yes. There it was.

She knew all those trips to the toilet had been for a reason. A little plastic bag. No need to check. She palmed it into her handbag and replaced it with her own little packet.

Karl missed his pot and shouted at Kev Trout, his wiry sidekick.

'Don't walk right fucking past me while I'm taking the fucking shot, Kev! Jesus Christ.'

Carol got up and potted the black, then shook Karl's hand. 'Thanks for the game, Karl.'

Karl leant in and whispered in her ear, 'Fancy a line, babes?'

'No, thank you. But you fill your boots. I won't tell.'

'Don't go anywhere,' he said, pointing at her then heading to the toilets, stopping off at his jacket on the way.

Carol sat at the bar and took a folded-up *Evening Standard* and a biro from her handbag.

'Go on. Give us a clue,' said Dennis, the bald and genial landlord.

'Four letters. Ending with D. "Perished".'

'Oof. Tricky one that,' said Dennis. 'But I know it.'

'You do?'

'Yes, love. Think I do, anyway.'

'All right, what is it?' said Carol. She liked Dennis. The world could do with more Dennises and fewer Karls. He pointed to her paper.

'"Dead".'

'DENNIS! CALL AN AMBULANCE!' Kev was running out of the toilets. 'I THINK KARL'S FUCKING KILLED HIMSELF!'

Carol looked down at her crossword and filled in three down, with pleasure.

FIVE

Ever been in a situation where you've made some lovely new friends but now they've all found out that you're a serial killer and you're worried they don't like you any more?

Carol started to get the feeling that something wasn't quite right when she went for her Saturday-morning coffee. A good way of appreciating the little things is to spend thirty-five years being denied them. Little things like a coffee on the bistro patio.

Now that she was free, Carol tried to enjoy everything Sheldon Oaks had to offer. On site there was a restaurant, a bar and a bistro, with a nicely kept outdoor eating area. Baking was just one of the activities. There was a pool, a gym, a yoga studio, a sauna, two tennis courts, boules (some French alternative to lawn bowling), a library with an 'arts and crafts' area, croquet on the front lawn, a snooker table and a cinema room. Silly, really, since half of the residents were virtually bedridden. Carol was sure that the climbing wall, for example, hadn't been used once. But you get what you pay for and everyone at Sheldon Oaks had paid rather a lot. 'Five-star comfort, five-star care.' That was their slogan and they delivered on it.

Carol was developing a habit of, after some toast in her apartment, heading down to the bistro and having a coffee outside. If lattes and cappuccinos and whatnot had been around before Carol had been imprisoned, they hadn't entered *her* life. She'd grown up a secondary-modern girl from South London. Tea and toast, egg and chips, 'Things were better when we had the Krays' – that was her world. After trying them all, she'd decided that Americano, with a splash of milk, one sweetener, was her drink of choice.

Carol was content to be on her own but usually, happily, somebody would end up joining her. Catherine might come over with a herbal tea and tell her about all the things she'd already done that day – a swim, a walk on the Heath, a video phone call with her grandchildren, a meeting with the charity she was a patron of. She really was the most unbearably perfect woman.

Or Margaret would sit down with crumbs from a croissant on her chest and deliver some gossip: Belinda from the second floor took a man back to her apartment the other night; Giles, the owner, seems to be rather aggressively selling – was he struggling for money? The home did seem to have a few empty apartments. The gardener, Tyler, smelt of drugs ('drugs' said in hushed tones with the same seriousness with which one might say 'suicide vest'). Did you know he's Elisa's son? Or the story, from the other night, which Margaret had heard second-hand, of Desmond having a stand-up row with Jim in the bar – 'You know, Carol, *Jim*, the chap who likes to sing.' Or the rumour, most likely triggered by Margaret's own paranoia, that if more people didn't start ordering vanilla cheesecake they might take it off the menu so, please, could everyone start treating themselves to it at least once a week.

This morning Carol had just ordered her coffee when Margaret had walked outside, seemed to jump, given a little shriek, then headed straight back indoors. It was as if she had seen a rat, but Carol felt as if what Margaret had in fact seen was *her*. Which reminded Carol that when she had passed Catherine in the lobby that morning, she had lifted her arm to wave and Catherine had flinched. Was Carol being paranoid?

Desmond was at a nearby table with his daughter and her husband, sharing a pot of tea. The two polo-shirted grandchildren stared at their tablets. Desmond hadn't noticed Carol and didn't look as if he would, so engaged were the three adults in a low-volume argument. Carol watched as Elisa skirted past Desmond and his family.

As she passed Carol, Elisa gave her a smile. 'Any plans for today, Carol?'

'No,' said Carol, smiling back.

'So you'll be staying at home for the day?'

'Oh, yes, I should think so, yes.'

'Good,' said Elisa, firmly, continuing on her way through the bistro. 'I want you to enjoy your time here.'

Would that be possible any more? Carol had been starting to feel so at home in Sheldon Oaks, so comfortable, that she hadn't even made herself a little shank for protection. Now, suddenly, something wasn't right. In prison, when things felt off, you worried someone was planning a hit on you. That seemed unlikely here.

With no plans for her Saturday, Carol had been hoping that

her morning coffee might present something. Perhaps Catherine would invite her for a walk, or maybe someone would suggest lunch in Hampstead. Now Carol felt an anxiety in the pit of her stomach. She resigned herself to going back to her apartment and making a start on the jumbo crossword book she'd bought from Ryman's yesterday.

Someone – was Polly her name? – had declined to enter the lift with her, her voice trembling as she said she'd take the stairs 'for the exercise'. Absurd, she thought. Carol's secret was definitely out. Polly had looked at her like she was an apparition, clinging on to her knitting for dear life. She was surely ninety, a little old lady who looked like a gust of wind could finish her off. Stairs were a far greater danger to Polly than entering the lift with a serial killer. Carol had only killed seven people! Maybe more ... She really should take a moment sometime to sit down and count them. But the point was, the vast majority of her hours had been spent *not* killing people. If Carol killed everyone she came into contact with she'd have no time for anything else. She hadn't killed *anyone* since the eighties ... apart from that guard someone else had taken the blame for.

Believe me, Polly, thought Carol, if I wanted you dead, I would have tripped you up in the first week. A firm handshake would probably have done the job.

Carol sat on her balcony and opened her puzzle book. A cleaner was vacuuming the hallway. The noise was irritating. Carol should have been out and about but now that she felt self-conscious it was as if she had retreated to her cell. If this was the way it was going to be, then this was the way it was going to be. People would grow to trust her.

The vacuuming stopped. Good. A gentle breeze, a touch of sun on her face. Hampstead was in the heart of North London but all she heard were birds in the trees. Carol Quinn was a lucky woman.

Go long enough without killing anyone and they'll see that those days are over. You're just Carol from baking now, she told herself. Death does not follow you around.

1 across. Group of crows (6).

Carol looked out, staring into the middle distance, trying to remember the word. Just then, something went directly past her eye line.

She stood up, took off her reading glasses and leant over her balcony. No one.

No one except a brand-new corpse, lying on the ground in front of the entrance.

A body, that seemed to fall straight out of the sky. It was raining the dead, as if Heaven was full and starting deportations.

'Hello?' Carol shouted. 'Is anybody there?'

She heard nothing but rapid footsteps, coming from above.

SIX

Well, this was fun. Carol had never seen a death she hadn't participated in herself before. She felt like Roger Federer must have felt the first time he'd gone to Wimbledon after retirement.

Ten minutes ago there had been no one outside. Now it seemed everyone was there, not wanting to miss out on the show. And what a show!

An ambulance, two police cars, the body still on the ground, dead on impact presumably. A young male police officer was carefully outlining the corpse in chalk.

'Jesus, you're not meant to be taking his inside leg. Just stick a circle round the poor bastard,' said a plain-clothes officer, who was about fifty and looked like a smoker. He turned to see Carol, who was waiting patiently beside him, and switched from copper mode to dealing-with-a-little-old-lady mode. 'Oh, hello there. Are you the lady who saw him fall?'

'Yes, that was me,' said Carol. 'He didn't fall. He was pushed. I heard footsteps.'

'Oh, is that right, is it? I see. I'm really sorry, madam, but can

I ask you to hang around for a moment? We'll want to talk to you. Do sit down, of course.'

He spoke in that way that people often do to older people: slower, louder, more pronounced, like they're talking to a toddler. Carol might understand it if she were ninety-five and wearing a nappy, being spoon-fed in a chair, not knowing what her own name was. But she wasn't ninety-five: she was seventy-five and she was doing absolutely fine, thank you very much. A sit-down did sound like a good idea, though.

Carol parked herself on a nearby wooden bench. Assorted residents stood in clusters, chatting, craning their old necks for a better view. Giles, the owner, buzzed around the paramedics, anxiously trying to hurry things along to no avail. Tyler, the young gardener, was sitting on a mower, watching, rolling himself a cigarette and mumbling to Viktor, the security guard, who had failed to prevent the only interesting incident to occur in his eight years on the job. Jill, the cleaner, edged out of the entrance and into the daylight. Jim, the gentleman who liked to sing in the bar, looked like he'd been headed for the lawn, croquet mallet in hand, but had stopped when he'd seen the drama. Belinda, dressed like the home's *femme fatale* in red lipstick and high heels – Jesus, it was barely afternoon yet – stared intently. Elisa was crying. Considering the demographics, surely residents died all the time? Not like this, Carol supposed. Normal folk weren't used to seeing a skull cracked open like an egg, its yolk all over the paving stones.

Carol looked up to the building's flat roof, where the body had presumably come from. He had to have been pushed. Those rapid footsteps above. The murderer's, surely.

'Is there anything I can help you with, gents?' Geoffrey was excitedly bounding over to the action.

'Stand back, please!'

'It's all right, copper. I'm one of you. DCI Geoffrey Standing, retired. I've been out of the game for a while so some of my methods may be a little out of date, but I'm sure I can help. Nothing changes really, does it? I take it you've already faxed the particulars over to all the local stations?'

'Thank you, sir.' It was the senior plain-clothes officer, heading Geoffrey off before he got to the body. 'You can help me by standing back.'

'Very good. That's exactly what you should be doing. Protect the crime scene. Like I say, though, I'm from the Met. What are we looking at? Suicide?'

'Really, sir. I need you to step away.'

'Excellent.' Geoffrey gave a chef's kiss before his shoulders slumped and he headed back towards Catherine and Margaret, dejected. He looked like a little boy who'd been told he couldn't join in with the bigger boys' game.

Carol was aware that the attention of many spectators was not on the body and the drama that surrounded it but on her. Everywhere she looked, glances were being flung in her direction. It dawned on her that in the minds of the people who knew her past, she was a suspect. How terribly *obvious* of them, she thought. Have a little imagination. Someone gets killed and the automatic assumption is that the known killer did it. If Jamie Oliver walks past a spaghetti carbonara, does that mean he cooked it?

If she were honest with herself, she could see the logic. *Had* she done it? It was possible, she supposed, that she had blacked out and, like some war veteran who finds himself transported to the battles of the past, murdered the man in a manic frenzy. To the best of her knowledge, she'd never done that before.

No. Surely not.

Not everyone was glancing at Carol. She noticed concern on the faces of the police around the body. Why? He was dead already. Dead is dead. What was there to be concerned about?

'Stand back, please.'

'Yes, excuse me.' Carol had returned. She needed a closer look at that corpse. Soon they'd all be gone and an opportunity would have passed. 'They said they'd want to speak to me. Do you happen to know when that might be? Only *Tipping Point* will be starting on ITV soon and I haven't missed an episode since it started.'

Playing up to the role of little old lady helped sometimes. A PC gave her a gentle smile. 'Just a moment. I'll ask for you.'

Carol could see her baking friends gawping at her. Just hours after her past had been discovered, here she was at the centre of a murder scene.

A younger female police officer, in a plain black suit, was talking to the older cop, whose face had turned from professional to grim. Something wasn't right. The body was on its side. A leg, broken at the hip, pointed in the wrong direction. The forehead had a circular imprint on it, like it had been hit by something round. Could Carol make out his face? Short white hair. The men here all had short white hair. With the police in deep conversation, Carol shuffled towards the corpse, leaning in, squinting.

'Lady. I need you to step back for me, please.'

The paramedics swooped in, covering the corpse with a sheet and stretchering it into the ambulance.

But Carol had her answer, not that she understood where all the fuss was coming from. She'd managed to figure out that the body belonged to Desmond from the baking group.

Poor Desmond.

But what had got the police so excited? What was so special about Desmond?

SEVEN

Young people were making their way from the tube station to the Heath, tote bags on their shoulders, stuffed with towels and sun cream and books they wouldn't get around to reading. Nice day for it. Inside the police car, DS Laura Welsh wished she was one of them.

'Pull over,' said DCI Bob Beattie.

'Where?'

'Anywhere. Pull over!'

'Okay.'

'Wait, don't. I can't do it here.'

'You want me to pull over or . . .?'

'Oh, Jesus . . .'

Bob started retching.

'I'll pull over.'

'DON'T PULL OVER!'

Laura had come to learn that men like Bob had a working-class respect for an upper-middle-class neighbourhood like Hampstead village. He couldn't allow himself to throw up outside a Gail's bakery.

'All right, all right, I won't.'

'Put the blues on.'

'Seriously?'

'PUT THE BLUES ON!'

The siren started. Laura got them through the red light, up the hill and away from the high street.

'Up here. Okay, pull over.'

Bob, the older, plain-clothes detective, the crumple-suited overweight cliché of a divorced man, jumped out and onto Hampstead Heath. Laura watched him from the lay-by as he proceeded to dive into the first bush he saw. She'd seen this kind of behaviour from Bob before. Usually, it would be the morning after a night when she'd left him and the other old tragics in the Wheatsheaf, ducking out before they hit the optics and pretended it was still the nineties and their bodies could take it. Why did they do it to themselves? Because it was all they knew? Habit? Were they running from their feelings? When it came to 'men's mental health' they'd got as far as putting some posters up around the station but no further.

Fair to say each of them who did the job they did had to face down a degree of the macabre. Laura enjoyed a post-work drink as much as anyone but it wasn't her crutch. When she wanted to escape the day's horrors, find some form of distraction, she found it in episode after episode of *Married At First Sight Australia* or *Below Deck*. She wasn't proud of it but she was comfortable with her vice. Pretty Australians having vacuous shouting matches in attractive locations was what got her through. It was a lot healthier than thirty units of alcohol and a Big Mac meal, which seemed to be Bob's method of facing down the demons.

Maybe if she stayed in the pub for longer she'd be making more progress. Still a detective sergeant, the game plan had been to be a detective inspector by now. She'd be a young one, but Laura was ambitious and not ashamed of it. Perhaps it was that people found her inherently funny. Her name was Laura Welsh but she was – get this – Scottish. Every new encounter in the force would start with peals of hilarity about her ironic name. It made her, she feared, a figure of fun rather than one of respect. She had two options: marry into a new surname or develop a Welsh accent. Neither was appealing.

Bob got back into the car, a drop or two of vomit on his shirt, which he wiped with his tie, pointlessly transferring the bile from one garment to another. Laura looked at him. This wasn't like a hangover. Bob's park pukes, on the odd occasion when they happened, were an early-morning thing. This was something else.

'Sorry,' he said.

Laura didn't move the car. In their year together she'd learnt how to play him. Give him a moment, she thought.

Bob stared in silence, then let out a guttural moan. 'This is bad. Fuck me, this is bad.'

Laura spoke quietly. This was serious. 'What?'

'You don't wanna know.'

But she did. Laura always wanted to know.

EIGHT

Margaret smiled at the baby in the café. It drooled on its mother's shoulder while she struggled to get something out of a bag full of baby-related paraphernalia. Sweet. Margaret looked around at people working on laptops, on their phones, a barista handling six orders at once, and it occurred to her that she was the least busy person in the building. Perhaps, she felt, the least busy person in London.

Margaret had arrived at the café on Hampstead High Street fifteen minutes early. The place had been Catherine's choice but Margaret wasn't sure if it was her scene. At least at Costa Coffee she knew where she was. Here it was all 'long blacks' and funny-looking pastries that cost seven pounds. The staff had interesting haircuts and tattoos that Margaret supposed were ever so fashionable that particular week. In her youth, tattoos had been the preserve of a certain type, a particular class. Now some of her friends' children had them. Middle-class people with middle-class jobs and anchors tattooed on their forearms. Was this what they called cultural appropriation?

She took in the decor. Industrial lighting, Bauhaus prints on the walls, cold grey tiling on the floor. As a trade minister, many years ago, Margaret had been on the odd trip to Communist East Germany. Who would have thought that the sort of aesthetic she'd found there would now be in a place that sold lemon-flavoured chocolate bars for eleven pounds?

She ordered herself a cup of tea and a 'cinnamon cronut' telling herself she deserved it after the day's dramatic events. Dear God, it did taste good. She wiped her mouth, looking around to see if anyone had noticed the size of her greedy first bite. Would she have another tea when the others arrived? That seemed a bit much, a tough assignment for the bladder. What if the others had cakes too? It would be hard to watch them eat theirs knowing that her fun was over.

Margaret was an early person, always had been. If you were early, you were on time; if you were on time, you were late; and if you were late, you were rude. She'd been almost militant about punctuality in her day, but was a lot more forgiving now.

Margaret had lived life at a rapid pace, fuelled by febrile ambition and then, suddenly, twenty-five years ago, that was all brought to an abrupt end. To be prime minister had been the goal. These days her mind was focused on tea intake and pastry pricing.

Now that she looked back, she wasn't even sure if she'd wanted to actually *do* the job. Prime minister! What an awful, awful life. Decisions, constant decisions, every one of them hard and every one of them guaranteed to enrage millions. The *responsibility*. As prime minister there was only one certainty: that you would at some point have to make a choice that would lead to someone's death. Denying funding for a vital medicine or approving one that went wrong. Ordering a military operation that directly killed someone or not ordering one that meant somebody, in some far-flung field, or perhaps – if you really cocked up – in your own country, would die. Every single person who managed to become prime minister had had to face the truth that their actions had ended people's lives. Except Liz Truss, who hadn't quite had the time.

Margaret had just wanted the achievement of getting the job. Tick! Do that and perhaps she could have told herself that her father, the man who had sent her off to boarding school at seven only to cruelly die when she was eight, would have been proud of her.

Margaret had once sat at the cabinet table in Downing Street, on a sweaty day in June, amid one crisis or another, after listening to each of her peers read out their (carefully tailored to achieve maximum personal advancement) contribution and thought: Every one of us is a deeply damaged person.

But that moment of clarity was brief and she had gone straight back to Britain's greasiest pole. Home secretary was the highest she rose. Not bad. Not quite top dog but one of the 'great offices of state'.

It had all come crashing down on an episode of *This Morning*. They were awful things, these friendly appearances on daytime television programmes. You'd prepare for a news interview like your career depended on it. Read and re-read the brief, load up all your little tricks, all your 'let me be clear's and 'I think what the public are interested in is ...'s. The rules were understood by all. Their goal was to get you to answer a question; yours was not to answer that question.

But *This Morning*, that was a shit-show waiting to happen. You had to do it, to reach all those normal people who didn't watch the news, but the trouble was that there was no way of knowing what you'd be asked. 'What's the price of a pint of milk?' That was the standard question, so you'd learn the answer to that. Ask any politician and they know the price of a pint of milk better than anyone. But anything could slip you up. Say the wrong thing about a TV soap and a nation would declare you 'out of touch' because you'd chosen to go to a state dinner with the German Chancellor instead of watching *Emmerdale*. *This Morning*, for a politician, was like Vietnam – the goal was to get out alive.

Margaret didn't.

The St Cuthbert's School Choir was singing some turgid cover for a charity Christmas single. That week Margaret had been dealing with a prison riot in Leeds, the police union had been getting greedy and were refusing a pay settlement, and she'd just received a report that some kind of sex maniac had been accidentally released and was last seen headed in the direction of Alton Towers. And here she had to sit and smile at the palest bunch of children she'd ever seen while they sang 'Frosty the Snowman'.

Still, she was nearly out of there. She'd got through her interview unscathed and now that the song was blessedly over, all she had to do was applaud like she meant it.

But then the host said, 'Actually, before we go to a break, I think Gavin has a question for you, Margaret.'

The boy was chubby, ginger and in a wheelchair. He spoke with a lisp. 'Why have you cut funding from Silly Sausages?'

What? Margaret fixed her grin. 'I'm sorry, I'm afraid I don't—'

'Silly Sausages. It's my local youth club. You've cut funding from it and now they don't have enough money to build a ramp for me.'

Margaret had absolutely no idea what he was talking about. It was almost certain that this had nothing to do with her or the government.

'I'm really sorry to hear that — was it Gavin? Yes, well, as I say, I'm really very sorry to hear that. This government has prioritised youth services because it's very important to us—'

The host chipped in. 'Obviously not enough to fund a ramp at Silly Sausages.'

Seriously, what on earth was Silly Sausages? 'As I say, funding is not always something that's set by central government, but I can certainly look into that for you. It sounds like a wonderful place.'

A tear rolled down Gavin's pale and freckled face. 'It *used* to be.'

'I'm afraid we'll have to go for a break there. Thank you very much to the home secretary for joining us.'

The host disappeared and Hugh, Margaret's aide, came over to get her out of there.

'Fat little shit,' mumbled Margaret. 'Honestly, I'm having a hard enough week as it is without getting Paxmanned by ginger Tiny fucking Tim. There was a time when an ungrateful little bastard like that would be locked in a district hospital and forgotten about.'

'Could I just grab your mic off you, please?'

It was the sound man.

Margaret's heart fell out of her chest and landed in her arse. 'Was this ... was this on?'

'Oh, I don't know. We're off air.'

Margaret spotted a floor manager with headphones on, staring at her. And then a producer. And then the director. They'd all heard it.

It led the six o'clock news that night. The bleeped tape was played, accompanied by an interview with the boy and his parents. It was as bad as bad could be. Gavin was an angel. That year he'd completed a fun run in his wheelchair to raise money for a local hospice. They showed pictures of him beaming in his medal with Margaret's words 'fat little shit' over the top. Jimmy Savile, then still a national treasure, was interviewed, saying Margaret had let her country down. She was fired before *News at Ten*.

Margaret had, she felt, done more good in office than bad. She had tried her best, but the sad truth was that, in the days before some of the current crop of politicians rewrote the rulebook, if you were broadcast calling a disabled eight-year-old a fat little shit on national television your career was over.

After Margaret had shot herself in the foot, made the goal she'd devoted every waking hour to an impossibility, her life got better. Freed from ambition she had the space to be, to her own astonishment, happy, and being happy gave her the space to be a nicer person. In short, with the constant pressure gone, she didn't call children fat little shits any more. Even when that was exactly what they were.

People stopped shouting at her in the street after about

three months. She made a few appearances on TV – *Celebrity Catchphrase*, *Celebrity Swim School* – as light entertainment, the scene of her death, became the scene of her resurrection. The public, who had always seemed to hate her, now liked her. A meaningless life was a virtuous one. Do nothing of any value, engage in only trivial things, and you will be rewarded for it.

Now she enjoyed her simple life in Sheldon Oaks. Baking, eating, gossiping. She hadn't opened a newspaper in years; her radio never left Magic Gold.

But lately she had noticed a restlessness. An itch. She wasn't dead yet but was she allowing herself to fade away? Was she in danger of drowning in shallow waters? She had a seat in the House of Lords but knew that politics was not, could not be, the answer. All the same, she needed something to sink her dentures into.

Geoffrey and Catherine entered and sat at her table.

Could this be it?

NINE

'All right, Catherine, Margaret. I'm going to write something down. Please be aware of our surroundings. We do not want to cause a scene.'

Geoffrey took a small police notebook from his inside jacket pocket. Margaret dabbed some cronut crumbs off her plate and put them into her mouth. As soon as Catherine's brownie had arrived, Margaret had wondered if she'd made the wrong choice.

Geoffrey wrote down one word, looked over his shoulder, then placed the notebook at the centre of the table for Catherine and Margaret to read.

'MURDER?' said Margaret.

'Sssh!'

She said it lower this time. '*Murder?*'

'Are we ruling out suicide?' asked Catherine. 'Or just a fall? Why murder?'

'I'm ruling nothing out.' Geoffrey took the notebook and scribbled again. He slowly slid it back to the centre of the table, revelling in the tension.

'CAROL? YOU THINK *CAROL* KILLED DESMOND?'

'I think perhaps, Geoffrey,' said Catherine, 'that if you just talk to us, rather than writing things down, then Margaret will stop yelling them out.'

Margaret leant forward, whispering this time, '*You think Carol killed Desmond?*'

'I think it's certainly a possibility. Here's what we know: deaths, at Sheldon Oaks, are not a rare occurrence. We are, all of us, in life's final chapter.'

'Really, Geoffrey,' said Catherine. 'I'd rather not dwell on that, if you don't mind. I feel I have a ways to go.'

'Your skin is looking lovely today, Catherine.'

'Thank you, Margaret.'

'Is it a cream?'

'Could be. I have some samples from Liberty, if you'd like.'

'It's diet, genes and a lack of direct sunlight,' snapped Geoffrey. 'Now, as I was saying, there are plenty of deaths at Sheldon but they're all pretty much the same. Natural causes or whatnot.'

'Strokes. Lot of strokes this year,' said Margaret.

'What *is* unusual is people falling off roofs. And our first such death comes when? Shortly after we gain a new resident who happens to be a convicted killer. And who is the first to supposedly witness that death? *That very same killer.*'

'Carol,' said Margaret, firmly, warming to his theme.

'I can see what you're saying, Geoffrey,' said Catherine. 'It seems a little bit of a stretch to me but you could be right. I'm sure that if she was involved the police will catch her soon enough.'

'Catherine. It gives me no pleasure to say this but the police force are, in my opinion, too woke to solve this crime. They should be at Sheldon Oaks right now, scouring the place for evidence, pinning Carol up against the wall, extracting the truth. But where are they? They're back at the station. Most likely putting the final touches on some rainbow flag bunting for their weekly parade. Or . . . or . . .' he scrambled, looking for another made-up scenario '. . . or practising a dance routine for the Notting Hill carnival or . . . or . . .'

'Geoffrey, is this because they wouldn't let you get involved?' asked Margaret.

'No! Absolutely not.'

'I think it is,' teased Catherine. 'I'm not sure I've ever seen a man look so sad.'

'They are failing to see what they have at their disposal,' said Geoffrey. 'A man on the inside!'

'So what are you suggesting?' asked Catherine.

'I think we should investigate it ourselves. This is important. If Carol did do it, then it's unlikely to be a one-off event, is it? Any one of us could be next.'

'I really don't think this is the sort of thing Margaret and I want to be getting ourselves involved in.'

'You speak for yourself,' said Margaret. 'I think I could have a lot to offer the investigation. And Geoffrey's right. We may need to act quickly before it turns into a . . . What's the word?'

'Killing spree?'

'Yes, that's it. Killing spree! We need to prevent a killing spree! Thank you, dear. We're ready for the bill now, if you are.'

The waitress cleared the table. Margaret thought she had seen her double-take at 'killing spree' but was far too excited to stop her train of thought. 'So what do you two think we should do, then?'

'Well, I think it's obvious,' said Geoffrey. 'We need to do what the police have thus far failed to do. Question the chief suspect.'

TEN

Americans were so over the top. Just kill people and be done with it. Why all the hullabaloo?

Since leaving prison, Carol had found herself enjoying true-crime documentaries. She was beginning to realise she had become a serial killer without, really, knowing anything of the genre. She was entirely self-taught. Carol wasn't one for letting her gender prevent her from doing what she wanted, but perhaps if she had known just how male-dominated the sport was she'd have paused before trying it.

Sex. So many of the other practitioners were obsessed with sex! For Carol, sex and murder just didn't go together. Like orange juice after brushing your teeth. Yuck. But it seemed that nearly everyone else who'd ever dabbled in a bit of multiple murder was killing and shagging like it was sausage and mash, which, she supposed, well, the way they did it, it was.

One channel, somewhere in the mid-hundreds showed episode after episode of one of those trashy American true-crime documentaries – *Women Who Kill*.

WOMEN WHO ... *KILL!* The bass-y, over-the-top American narrator would say every five minutes or so.

Then they'd tell the story of some lady in Kansas who'd finally lost it with her husband and shot him with his own Colt .45. You'd watch the police interrogations with the women and they'd be crying, saying sorry, saying they loved him, saying they'd lost their mind.

Own it, thought Carol. These men had all beaten the shit out of their wives or cheated on them or stolen their money. The bastards deserved it. *Own it.*

One time Carol had been sitting in a train carriage, with only a disgusting slob for company. He had belched loudly and proudly. Scratched his arse, farted the most awful farts. He had been proud of it. He'd known she was behind him. This was an intentional assault on her person. He'd done it because he'd enjoyed it, because it had made him feel big and because he'd known he could get away with it.

At least, he'd thought he could.

Carol had seen the station approach and slowed her breathing, slotting herself into the appropriate state. She'd taken a newly sharpened flick-knife from her coat pocket, released the blade and pushed it into the back of his neck.

By the time the train had arrived at the platform, Carol was standing by the doors, looking directly into the man's eyes, his life already leaving him.

He was pleading with her. *What have you just done?*

'Don't burp in front of ladies,' she'd said, in a motherly tone. 'It's rude.'

*

Carol heard a knock and went to her front door to find Geoffrey, Catherine and Margaret staring at her. They each had a defensive weapon in hand. Geoffrey held a cricket bat, Catherine a sock with a snooker ball in it, and Margaret a large cookery book.

WOMEN WHO ... *KILL!* came booming from the living room.

'Oh, hello,' said Carol.

A flustered Margaret spoke first. 'Oh, hello, Carol. I've got ... I just remembered that I've got this lovely big Mary Berry book and I wondered, well, I was wondering if you might like to go through a few of the recipes with me. You know, to see if we'd like to try one out this Friday.'

'I see. And why are you here, Geoffrey? To practise your batting? Would you like me to bowl you a few deliveries?'

'We'd like to ask you a few questions,' said Catherine.

'You've formed a murder club, haven't you?'

No one spoke.

'Don't be shy! You've formed a murder club! I'm pleased for you.' Carol had heard about them popping up all over the place. In retirement homes, pub quiz teams. Apparently there was even one in Marlow. CCTV was bad enough. Sticking a knife into a man's neck on a train without anyone seeing would be a right faff nowadays. Time was when a murderer only had to worry about the police. Now everyone with a minute to spare was an amateur sleuth, watching your every move.

'Well, please, come in. Would you like me to take your snooker ball in a sock for you, Catherine, or do you want to keep hold of it, you know, for safety?'

'Um ... I'll just put it in my handbag, if that's okay.'

'Lovely. Tea? Coffee?'

The four of them sat around Carol's kitchen table sipping tea. No one had said much since the business at the door.

'So, I'm guessing you've all realised I used to be a serial killer and now you think I killed Desmond. Is that right?'

Catherine cleared her throat. 'We don't know what we think. Desmond may simply have fallen.'

'Or it could have been suicide,' said Margaret.

'Did Desmond look to you like a man who was about to kill himself?' asked Carol. 'He was always in a good mood and Friday was no different.'

'True,' said Geoffrey.

'People can be very good at hiding their true mental state,' said Margaret. 'There was a programme about it on Radio 4 the other morning but I had to switch back to Magic Gold because I didn't like the presenter's voice.'

'Desmond didn't kill himself,' said Carol.

'And how do you know that?' asked Catherine.

'Because he was murdered.'

The air thickened.

'Not by me, but I'm guessing my saying that won't be enough to persuade you, what with my history. It's sad, really. There are some things that people just really struggle to get past. Do stop shaking, Margaret. Would you be more comfortable if I kept my hands on the table at all times? Like this?'

'How do you know he was murdered?' asked Geoffrey. 'What makes you so sure?'

'My apartment is directly below where he fell. I was sitting on the balcony. Immediately after his tumble, which I happened to see, by the way, I heard someone running on the roof. I'm not a professional investigator like yourself, Geoffrey, and I'm not a part of any murder clubs like you, Margaret and Catherine, but that, to me, seemed awfully like it was the murderer. What we need to find out is *how* Desmond got onto the roof and *why* Desmond got onto the roof. Was he led there? If so, by who ...' Geoffrey shuffled. 'Sorry, Geoffrey, by *whom*.'

The room was still.

Carol broke the silence. 'Of course, you'll want to eliminate me from your enquiries, I'm sure.'

'Well, if you don't mind, that would be nice. Do you have a ... What's the word?'

'Alibi? No. Afraid not. I was sitting on the balcony, but you'd have to take me at my word for that and I'm getting the impression that my word isn't quite enough right now.'

'We're very sorry,' said Catherine. 'It's just ...'

'I know, I know. Isn't it always "just"? Nothing's ever easy. This is how I see it. The only way I'm going to get off the hook here is if I can find the murderer and clear my name.'

'That's the long and the short of it, I suppose, yes,' said Geoffrey.

'Very well. Then I guess it is what it is. I'd better get cracking. We'd probably work better as a team but I'm getting the sense you don't want me in your club just yet. It's a shame because I think we could be phenomenal. A former detective, a former home secretary, a former doctor and me, someone with a bit of practical experience. If we could stay friends, somehow, I'd appreciate it.'

'Of course!' said Margaret, surprising both Geoffrey and Catherine a little.

'I promise not to murder any of you. Not unless you get on my wrong side, that is.'

The new murder club laughed awkwardly.

'Boo!'

Margaret nearly fell off her chair.

'Sorry,' Carol said, holding up her hands. 'Really, I promise. My murdering days are over. To tell you the truth, I just don't have the energy any more.'

'All right. Well, I think we ought to . . .' Geoffrey stood up.

'I understand, Detective Chief Inspector. You have a lot of work to do.'

He blushed at being called what he hadn't been called in a long time. They all gathered their things and headed towards Carol's front door.

'Couple of things you might want to think about,' said Carol.

'Oh, yes?'

'Well, I managed to get a glimpse of Desmond's face before they took his body away. There was an indentation on his forehead that didn't look, to me, like it came from the fall. He looked like he'd been hit by something distinctive that had left an imprinted circle.' She looked at Geoffrey. 'Not a cricket bat, for example, so you're out of the picture, Geoffrey. Something else.'

'Thank you,' said Catherine. 'That's, uh, very useful.'

'Catherine, you were a doctor, weren't you?'

'Pathologist, actually, but, well, yes,' said Catherine.

'Hang on,' said Carol, pointing at each of them in turn.

'Detective, home secretary, pathologist. This is absurd. How is this place so full of criminal investigators?'

Catherine, Margaret and Geoffrey looked at each other. Catherine offered a possible reason: 'Word of mouth?'

'I think it's just one of those funny things,' said Margaret. 'You could say that having an ex-murderer here at least balances the place out a bit.'

Carol gave a polite laugh then picked up her train of thought. She pointed at Catherine. 'What's your view on poison?'

'What do you mean?'

'Well, if, say, you had put some arsenic in each of your friends' tea, how long should you expect to have to wait before they all stop breathing?'

Margaret immediately started wheezing and held onto the back of a chair for support. Geoffrey's arm slowly rose in horror, his finger directing itself at Carol, who laughed.

'Joke! It's a joke!'

Margaret's relief turned to laughter. 'Oh, dearie. Oh, dearie me.'

'If I was going to get back to it, I wouldn't be fooling around with poison. Poison is boring. Much better to crack an axe into someone's skull.'

Margaret broke the silence. 'Well, thank you for the chat. It's been lovely to see you.'

'You too. Be safe out there,' said Carol. 'There's a murderer about.'

ELEVEN

Carol turned the handle and shook the door. Locked. It had been an effort to get up the steps.

Beside the lift doors on her floor, the top floor, there were doors to the stairs. As far as she could tell, this was the only entry to the roof. Police tape had been stretched over it in an X.

'You lost?'

She turned. It was Tyler, the scruffy teenage gardener, Elisa's son.

'You ain't supposed to go up there.'

'Why is it locked?'

'Dunno. Police don't want no one up there. Crime scene, innit?'

'Yes, but, I mean ... why is there a lock at all? Isn't that unusual? You could lock somebody up there, if you wanted to. I would have thought that wasn't allowed.'

'Dunno. That's the way they wanted it.'

'You fitted the lock?'

Tyler grunted in the affirmative.

'Who asked you to fit the lock?'

'D'you want me to help you back to your apartment?'

'I want you to tell me who asked you to fit that lock.'

Tyler looked over his shoulder, then spoke with menace. 'I ain't gotta tell you nuffin'.'

Carol narrowed her eyes. If she had a trigger, it was bad manners. She and Tyler were close enough that she could land a head-butt on the bridge of his nose, then slam her heel into his foot. That would be enough for her to gain the upper hand. If she was carrying a weapon, she could finish him there and then.

Carol was shaken out of her violent fantasy by a female voice, echoing down the corridor.

'Can I help you? Are you a little lost?' It was Elisa, the concierge.

'Oh, sorry,' said Carol. 'I sometimes get a bit confused.'

'Oh, Carol, don't worry. Let me help you down those steps.'

'It's like a maze in here. This young man was being so helpful.'

'Thank you, Tyler,' said Elisa, placing a hand on her son's shoulder. Tyler flinched, still young enough to be embarrassed by a touch from his mother, and scarpered. Elisa took Carol by the arm and led her towards the corridor. 'I was just about to knock on your door, actually. I'm sure you heard about what happened.'

'I saw him fall.'

'Oh, yes, I did hear about that, yes. Now, I don't want anybody to worry but the police are coming to speak with us all at five o'clock today. In the hall.'

'Oh, I see.'

'They probably just want to put everybody's minds at ease.'

'Oh, that's nice.'

'Were you friendly with Desmond?' asked Elisa. 'You were in the baking group together, weren't you?'

'Oh, I suppose I knew him a little. Lovely man. Did you know him at all?'

They stopped at Carol's door. Elisa sighed. 'Desmond? Did I know Desmond? Um . . . no. Not really. I don't think I ever did.'

TWELVE

Bob Beattie inhaled on his cigarette as if he was trying to down it all in one go.

'I thought you were giving up,' said Laura.

'That was vaping. I said I was giving up vaping.'

'Oh, well, that's okay, then.'

They were in the sparsely populated car park of Sheldon Oaks at the rear of the building. A Jaguar, an Audi, a new Mini, their own unmarked Vauxhall Corsa.

'Nice place this,' said Laura. 'Sure it costs more than we'll ever be able to afford.'

'It's not bad. My mum stays here,' said Bob. 'They keep her busy enough.'

Laura turned to him in surprise, the question 'How do you afford it?' implied in her look.

'I got a good deal,' said Bob, returning to his cigarette.

An old oak tree at the back of the car park took up much of the sky, its trunk thick, huge branches all winding on their individual journeys, hundreds of years in the making.

Laura tried not to get bothered that she was packing her own sandwiches every morning yet Bob was somehow able to find enough spare cash to send his mother to a place like this. Laura thought of the old detective who'd tried to stick his beak in at the crime scene. Geoffrey? How had he ended up with enough cash to retire to a place like this when he'd been on a police salary? Probably bought his house for a fiver and a bag of potatoes in 1975 and sold it for ten mill last year. That's the way it seemed to go in London. The idea of Laura ever getting on the housing ladder was fanciful.

Giles, the ruddy-cheeked owner, stepped out from behind the fire door. 'That's everybody, I think. Everyone who's mobile, anyway.'

'Thank you,' said Laura.

'I was thinking,' said Giles. 'Do we really need to say that the death was suspicious?'

'It was,' said Bob, deadpan.

'Yes, I appreciate that's what your line of thinking is but ... you're not a hundred per cent *certain*, are you? Personally I think it was most likely just a fall and, well, this *is* a group of elderly people. Do we really want to upset them unnecessarily?'

'In my experience it's always best to be as honest with people as you can be,' said Bob. 'I'm sure you agree with that, Giles?'

'Certainly. Yes. Certainly. Up to a point.'

'Good.'

They entered what Giles called 'the ballroom', where the residents had gathered. At the edge there was a long, shiny modern bar with angular chrome bar stools and gold-framed paintings of Victorian hunting scenes. The blend of styles didn't work. Sheldon Oaks didn't quite know what century it belonged in. But neither did some of the residents so maybe that was fair enough, thought Laura.

Tyler was finishing off arranging rows of chairs for the old folks. There was a hum of excited murmurs, like when someone famous comes to speak at a school assembly. Some of the Sheldon Oaks staff, a couple of chefs, some waiters, a cleaner, were standing at the back of the room. Bob received a kiss on the cheek from an old lady, his mum presumably, then joined Laura by the wooden stage. His face was red, still not too old to be embarrassed by public affection from his mother.

'All good?' Giles asked the two police officers. They nodded.

Laura noticed Bob nervously digging dirt from underneath his fingernails. 'Don't make any jokes,' she mumbled, under her breath.

Carol watched Giles step onto the stage and approach the microphone. He looked sweaty.

'Hello, everybody. Thank you for coming together at such short notice. I think I'll get straight to it. A couple of police officers have very kindly asked to speak to you all today so I'll just hand things over to the detective chief inspector.'

Carol sat alone at the back of the hall. She smiled at Geoffrey, Catherine and Margaret but kept a respectful distance. The smiles they gave in return were those thin non-smiles, the type you might send in the general direction of a car when walking over a zebra crossing. Two of the older residents got close to sitting next to Carol, then spotted her and jumped, turning on their heels as fast as it was possible for octogenarians to do. This was becoming tiresome.

Bob stepped up to the microphone. He looked nervous, Carol thought.

'What's got loads of balls and screws old ladies?'

The room was silent.

'Bingo ... because of the ... Sorry. Hello. I'm Detective Chief Inspector Bob Beattie. This is DS Laura Welsh and don't worry ... *She's not actually Welsh.*'

Carol noticed her almost put her head into her hands.

DCI Beattie ploughed on. 'Sorry, I didn't mean to offend anyone. I just thought you might like a little joke. Sorry. Right. As you've all no doubt heard, one of your number, Sir Desmond Crisp, died yesterday.'

Sir Desmond Crisp? Not surprising, really, considering the pedigree of many of the other residents, but what had he been knighted for? It occurred to Carol that she'd never asked what Desmond did.

'Now, the good thing is that at this point, if you were a younger group of people, I'd now probably have to say something about how counselling is available to anyone who needs it, but I won't be doing that today because your generation just gets on with things, don't you? You beat the Nazis. You're not going to cry over this.'

'Most of us were actually born after the war,' said Geoffrey, from the audience.

'Oh? Is that right? Yeah, didn't think of that. Yeah, I suppose you were. I'm talking bollocks, aren't I? Shit. Didn't mean to swear. Fuck!'

'Get to the point, Bob,' said Laura, leaning across from the edge of the stage.

'Sorry. Right. Sorry, I'm really not used to public speaking. They had a course down the nick but I was off with gout that week. You'd think gout was gone now. I thought it was from the Victorian times, you know, but nope, you can still get it. Too much red meat apparently. Fucking painful. Shit. Sorry.'

'*Bob!*'

'Should have let you do this, shouldn't I, Laura? Problem with women is if you give them an inch, they take a mile. Am I right, fellas? *I cannot stop!* Right. Sorry. Okay.' Bob made a show of composing himself and adopting a professional mode. 'We have reason to believe that Sir Desmond's death may have been suspicious.'

There were shocked murmurs from some in the room.

'I know!' said Bob. 'But that's what we're dealing with so—'

'Was it an illegal immigrant?' asked Agatha, one of the older residents, with a shaky voice.

'What was that, Mum?'

'Was it an illegal immigrant? Usually is.'

'Sorry, that's my mum there. Agatha. I'm sure you all know her. We're not going to reveal anything with regards to suspects just now.'

'Ah!' said Agatha. 'So it was. I knew it!'

'As I say, well … Actually, I'm just going to nip that one in the bud. We have no reason to believe that it was an illegal immigrant.'

'They're sneaky!' said Agatha, not letting the matter go.

Bob tried to get things back on track. 'Okay. Well, what I wanted to say was this. If anyone has any information at all, if anyone saw anything suspicious—'

'There's a black man who works in the restaurant,' said Agatha.

'Thank you, Mum. Uh . . . yep. We'll, er, we'll look into that.' Bob shook his head to indicate to the rest of the room that they wouldn't be looking into that. 'I'm going to leave you all one of these.' Bob held up a piece of paper.

'It has DS Welsh's and my details on it. And if you have anything, anything at all . . .' Bob looked at Agatha '. . . well, maybe not *anything* but, yes,' he turned back to the rest of the room, 'do get in touch. We'd be very interested in speaking to you. That's everything for now, I think. Thank you for your time.'

'I have a question.' Carol had her hand raised.

Bob, who had already started to edge off the stage, relieved it was all over, returned to the microphone. 'Yes?'

'How should we protect ourselves? You're saying there's a murderer about, yes?'

'Uh, I'm saying it's a possibility. We've no reason to suspect they want to harm anybody else.'

'And you've no reason to suspect they don't. I'm told some people like to kill for fun.'

'All right.' Giles hopped onto the stage with a reassuring smile. 'You're all very safe. Don't worry. Derek will look after us.'

The room looked at Derek, the Sheldon Oaks security guard, who was slouched in a comfy chair by the wall. Upon hearing his name he jolted himself out of his nap. He was overweight, had a mop of white hair and thick glasses. No one had ever seen him move. Derek, thought Carol, might well be the oldest person in the room.

'I have something to say.' Belinda, one of the residents, was wearing big dark sunglasses and a fur coat. She had a kind of cheap glamour, like the mother of a millionaire boxer. 'If anybody has been wondering why I'm wearing sunglasses it's because I've been crying so much.'

'Oh,' said Giles. 'Well, thank you, Belinda.'

'Over Desmond. That's the reason I've been crying. Because Desmond is . . .' she started to wail '. . . *deeead!* Oh, oh, I can't do this.'

'All right, we'll just wrap things up there, then,' said Bob.

Belinda stood up and projected her voice, performing to the whole room. 'I'd like it to be known that I cannot be the murderer because I loved Desmond and he . . . oh, oh, this is so painful . . . he loved me. Why? Why did he have to die? *Whyyyyy?*'

Inside Carol's white Reeboks, her toes curled.

Geoffrey stood up. 'Hello. DCI Geoffrey Standing. CID. Is yourself aware that one of the residents at Sheldon Oaks is a convicted serial killer?'

Bob Beattie looked to his colleague and Giles took control of the microphone. 'Thank you, Geoffrey. I think the police can deal with things from here on in.'

'Thank you, Giles, but I *am* the police,' said Geoffrey. He pointed to Carol. 'Carol Quinn. Over there. Served thirty five years for seven murders. Her MO – which, as you'll know already, officers, but just for everyone else in the room, is a phrase that we police use that stands for "modus operandi" – her MO was murder, simply for the pleasure in it. In layman's terms, Carol Quinn is a psychopath. I suggest you bring her in for questioning.'

Carol wanted desperately to defend herself but worried that any sign of a temper might serve only to affirm Geoffrey. 'I'm not a psychopath,' she said, too quietly for anyone to hear.

'I have a question.'

Carol turned to see a chef, a handsome man in his thirties, with slicked-back black hair and an Italian accent, his hand up.

'Uh, yes?' said Bob Beattie, clearly impatient to leave.

'If the police won't lock Miss Carol up now, maybe we can do it here. Lock her in her room, yes?'

'I don't recommend ...'

Giles interrupted Beattie. 'We won't be doing that. Everyone is equal in the Sheldon Oaks family.'

Now the cleaner spoke up. 'Why's she here anyway? I should talk to the union. This can't be right. Where does it say in the contract that we have to clean up after murderers?'

'Maybe,' Norma, a tiny ninety-something lady in a wheelchair, spoke up, 'we should check if any of Carol's semen was found on the body. Isn't that usually how they do it on *Forensic Files*?'

Bob returned to the microphone. 'We will, of course, be looking into any possible leads. In the meantime, I suggest that you are all, uh, vigilant, and I'm sure that, uh,' he looked to the barely alive security guard, 'Derek will take care of you all.'

As the stage cleared, Carol had the sense that the atmosphere had turned from moderate excitement to all-out fear, and she was the cause.

Bob and Laura were walking slowly back to the Corsa. As far as Bob was concerned, they were done for the day. Leyton Orient were playing at home that night. He had time for a couple of pints before kick-off. Needed them.

'You know Carol Quinn?' asked Laura.

'Know *of* her. Before my time. I'm not *that* old.'

'Shouldn't we be questioning her now?'

'Let's do the autopsy first, shall we? Would be handy to have something to throw at her.'

'What if she kills someone else?' said Laura.

'We'll just have to cross that bridge when we come to it.'

'You worked with Des Crisp, right?' asked Laura.

'Not with him, really. I was still a baby bill when he left. Knew him a bit.'

'What was he like?'

'Oooof,' exhaled Bob.

'Are the rumours true?'

'Trust me, Laura, you don't want to know.'

Laura got into the car and waited for Bob to get in at the passenger side.

'What if I do? What if I do want to know?' she said, as Bob strained with the effort of sitting down and shut his door.

Bob threw his cigarette out of the window and popped some nicotine gum into his mouth. 'He was scum. And now we've got to clean up his mess.'

Laura growled. 'Now we've got to clean up his mess.'

'What?'

'Never heard that one out loud before.' She went into the character of 'grizzled old cop'. 'He was scum, kid. Scum. And now we've got to clean up his mess.'

Bob laughed. Playing along, he attempted a New York accent. 'Now we gotta clean up his mess.'

'I got enough mess of my own. Now I gotta clean up this punk's mess too?'

They went silent, each deciding the joke had run its course.

'Maybe he did just fall off,' said Laura.
'Wouldn't that be lovely?'

Carol stayed in her chair, stewing, while the other residents shuffled out. She'd tried to blend in, just to be another person, and she'd failed. As a child, she'd never really felt like one of the other children. At thirteen she'd moved schools and seen it as a chance to restyle herself as a 'normal girl', wearing what they wore, talking how they talked, but it hadn't worked. Kids can tell.

Now it had happened again. All because she was a murderer. All that finger-pointing, all those accusations: it had hurt. Maybe she should embrace the role, stop pretending, be who she was. She'd never killed a whole roomful of people at once. Just a few minutes before, when all the eyes had been on her, if there had been a button that could have extinguished the lot of them, melted them, turned them into nothing more than puddles on the floor, would she have pressed it? Tempting.

While it was on her mind, Carol took her phone from her handbag and googled 'Sir Desmond Crisp'. She immediately saw a picture of him in uniform that looked about thirty years old. He appeared harder, steelier, more cynical. Not like the cuddly, retired Desmond she'd known.

Below the picture was a caption: 'Sir Desmond Crisp. Former head of the Metropolitan Police.'

She smiled at the absurdity of it. Trust her to go to a retirement home packed with ex-police.

THIRTEEN

Catherine smiled at Marco, the square-jawed waiter. 'Can I get you something to drink?' he asked.

'I'm sure my friends won't be long.' Catherine thought she had to start dragging the others out once in a while. The fancy café with the tattooed staff was as adventurous as it had got. They were in London, for Heaven's sake. Hampstead was on their doorstep, with its charming little Italian restaurants, and Vietnamese and Indian and Greek and Lebanese and Turkish, and yet when they ate together they always ate here, in the home's onsite restaurant, the Apple Tree. It felt sanitary to Catherine, as if everything had been bought from a website called restaurantfurniture.com. They could have been in a four-star chain-hotel restaurant anywhere in the world. It had no character.

There was also the fact that every one of the diners was elderly. Catherine was to blame, of course. She'd *chosen* to be here but she'd retired from work, not the world. She had not intended to sequester herself like this. She was an old person and she was in an old person's development but that wasn't all she was. She'd have liked to be around young people too and yet she'd voluntarily hidden herself away from them.

It was all Nigel's fault, of course. Bastard. They'd always planned on retiring to the South of France together. They'd never got as far as buying a place, but Annecy looked nice. Catherine had even been brushing up on her French in preparation, diligently hitting her targets on the app on her phone.

Then Nigel left her.

For a younger woman.

On Christmas Day.

Bastard.

Everyone agreed that Nigel was making a fool of himself, he was being an idiot, embarrassing, 'a total wally' was a common phrase. And they were right but that didn't make it any less heartbreaking. Heartbreak, actual heartbreak, in her mid-seventies. She was prepared for grief – with Nigel's diet she'd thought it inevitable that he'd go first – but heartbreak? It was ridiculous.

Emily was her name. Fiftyish, blonde, pretty but in a way, Catherine thought, that you could tell she put rather a lot of effort into it. What galled Catherine most was how Emily reduced *her*. Catherine had been blonde and pretty in her day, still got compliments now, but that wasn't *all* she was. She was a doctor and a mother and bloody good company, actually. All this time, despite everything she'd achieved, had she been nothing more than a trophy wife to Nigel? Sure, they'd had fun together, good conversations, some lovely children, some lovely holidays, but ultimately once the wrinkles had set in and the hair had gone grey, had she lost her value in his eyes? Like one of his stocks?

Bastard.

So Sheldon Oaks had seemed like a good choice. She didn't want to be alone, didn't want to be the old lady on the street everyone smiled at but never spoke to. Didn't want to be a burden on her children. Jack, her eldest, had suggested here and Catherine wasn't too proud to see that it made sense. Still in London, near two of her three kids, pleasant, close to theatres and whatnot and with its own little community.

'Sorry we're late,' said Margaret, waddling up to the table and putting down her handbag. 'We bumped into each other in the foyer and there was an electrician fixing something and Geoffrey started explaining to him how to rewire a plug and why British plugs are the best in the world.'

'They are,' said Geoffrey, sitting down. 'Nothing will make you more patriotic than an American socket. Evening, Catherine.'

'Evening.'

They ordered and ate. Cod for Catherine, chicken for Margaret, lamb for Geoffrey, a bottle of sauvignon blanc between them, of which Geoffrey had the bulk.

Belinda's performance in the hall was the first topic of conversation.

'Did you know that they were an item?' asked Catherine.

'I'm not sure they were,' said Margaret. 'Not exclusively, anyway. Belinda seems to have worked her way through every gentleman here.'

'Not this one,' said Geoffrey, proudly.

'I bet you would, though, wouldn't you?' said Catherine.

'Please. My years of carnal desire have long gone.' Then, after a pause for consideration, Geoffrey conceded, 'Yes, probably.'

'Urgh, honestly,' said Catherine. 'You disappoint me.'

'Is she on our list of suspects, do we think?' said Margaret.

'You can start a list, if you like, but I'm telling you now, Carol did it,' said Geoffrey.

Catherine frowned. 'That seems like a rush to judgement. I can see why she's a suspect, a big one, but we don't actually have any evidence, do we? Geoffrey, I felt a little sorry for her when you spoke about her in the hall.'

'Trust me. When you were in the game as long as I was, you learnt to spot the murderer. All we have to do now is construct a case against her.'

'And how many convictions did you have overturned, Geoffrey?' asked Margaret, pointedly.

Geoffrey mumbled.

'Say it a little louder, Geoffrey. I don't think Catherine heard you.'

'Eleven.'

'If it's all the same to you, I'm going to withhold judgement for a little longer,' said Margaret.

Marco, the waiter, arrived.

Geoffrey, affronted, got in one childish jab. 'She did it.'

'Would you like to see the dessert menu?'

Margaret feigned disinterest. 'I mean, I don't . . .'

'No, thank you,' said Catherine and Geoffrey, simultaneously, and Margaret's shoulders slumped.

'Have a dessert, if you like, Margaret,' said Catherine.

'No, no, no. I'm fine. I'm fine.'

'I take it you both read Desmond's obituary in *The Times*,' said Catherine.

Margaret and Geoffrey both mmmed, suggesting, to Catherine, that there was more to say.

'Did you know him, Geoffrey?'

'That I did, that I did.'

'I knew him too,' said Margaret, with a conspiratorial smile.

'Oh, yes?' said Catherine.

'Geoffrey, what did you think of Desmond?' asked Margaret. 'Not in here. I mean when you worked with him.'

Geoffrey checked that nobody else was listening in before he spoke ill of the dead. 'It doesn't feel right saying this, not now, but Desmond was corrupt.'

'That's why I asked,' said Margaret. 'I heard allegations in the Home Office.'

'What kind of allegations?' asked Catherine, leaning forward.

'Well, I don't know,' said Margaret. 'Just murmurs. I think I asked them to put it into a report for me but nobody wanted to write anything down. Honestly, it was impossible to get anything done. Ever.'

'He was on the payroll,' said Geoffrey. 'Couple of the big London organised-crime gangs. The people at the top paid him to turn a blind eye. The foot soldiers, they'd still get cuffed, but the ones at the top, he had them covered.'

'I never really thought about it,' said Catherine. 'Sounds like something from a film, but of course that sort of thing happens, I suppose.'

'The world isn't all roses, I'm afraid, my dear Catherine,' said Geoffrey, as if he were speaking to a grandchild.

I know that perfectly well, thought Catherine. I was a pathologist. I've seen things that would turn you green. But she let it slide. Geoffrey meant well and something had just occurred to her.

'Wasn't Jim, the chap who likes to sing, wasn't he a bit of a . . .' she lowered her voice '. . . *criminal?*'

'Jim. Oh, yes, he most certainly was. Top of the tree in his day. Ran North London for a time,' said Geoffrey.

'Lovely voice. Charming man. Shame about the crime,' said Margaret.

'And was he paying Desmond off, do you think?' asked Catherine.

Geoffrey was looking away, into the middle distance, his mind on another time, Catherine supposed. They all had pasts.

'I couldn't say for sure but it would surprise me if he wasn't.'

Margaret looked at Catherine. They were having the same thought at the same time. The three of them were leaning in together now in conspiracy, their heads nearly touching at the centre of the table. Catherine spoke first. 'Jim and Desmond had a shouting match the other night,' she said.

'Did they now?' said Geoffrey. 'What about?'

'Yes! They did!' said Margaret, excited. 'I saw it! I don't know what they were arguing about but they were both rather animated. I'd never seen Desmond like that before. He was always so lovely and placid at baking.'

'Let me introduce you to a little saying,' said Geoffrey. 'There's more to some people than meets the eye.'

'Thank you, Geoffrey,' said Catherine, deadpan. 'I'd never heard that one before.'

'Surely you'd both agree that Jim requires looking into,' said

Margaret. 'I mean, an ex-criminal, who was seen arguing with the victim a couple of nights before the murder.'

'I suppose it wouldn't do any harm to question him,' said Geoffrey. 'He plays croquet most mornings. We could approach him then, although I do insist on taking the lead.'

'We can't do it tomorrow morning. We're busy.' Catherine sat back. Time to give them her news. She surprised herself with how excited she was. 'I still keep in touch with a few old colleagues and, well, I managed to get us tickets to Desmond's autopsy.'

Margaret clapped her hands together and let out a yelp of delight. 'Oh, come on, let's have dessert to celebrate!'

FOURTEEN

It was a few seconds before Carol remembered she wasn't waking up in a cell. The light shone into her room, not in vertical lines but horizontal. Blinds, not bars. There was no smell of piss and bleach. No fluorescent strip lighting. The city traffic sounded like peaceful ocean waves.

Half awake, she saw Desmond's lifeless body on the ground, his face oddly peaceful. That imprint, a neat circle, on his forehead. Was she remembering it right? Still in bed, she rolled herself into the position in which they'd found him. Strange for her, as a perpetrator, to momentarily occupy the role of victim. Desmond was lying on his left side. Carol put her hand to her head, *his* head in her imagination. The wound she'd seen was on the right side of the forehead.

Now Carol changed part. She got onto all fours in her bed, and held an invisible weapon over her head. She was back in the role she was born to play. She pictured Desmond's helpless body below her, right where she had been, and slowly landed her pretend blows. They were landing on the left side of his forehead. She, a right-hander, was hitting the *left* side of his forehead.

Now she changed hands, passing her imaginary weapon between them. She held up the weapon again, but now in her left hand. It felt wrong. Her blows came down with no force and no accuracy. It was icky. Just a switch of the hands had turned her from accomplished assassin to a toddler with a hammer.

The wound was on the right side of Desmond's forehead. The murderer was left-handed.

She chose to skip coffee downstairs and opted for a cup of Kenco instant on her balcony. The grass was green, the sun shone bright, her time was her own. All those years in prison and the world had been out here, happily carrying on without her.

Before Carol was locked up she had loved a morning walk in Burgess Park, South London, especially in summer. People on their way to work, joggers, alkies and school kids sharing the same space. In London, you were never more than a few feet from a millionaire and a crackhead, and back when Pete Doherty from the Libertines was in his prime, you could find both housed in the same person.

One morning, Carol had seen a man kick his dog, hard, teeth clenched, like he meant it. It had stopped her in her tracks. She had enough distance and he was in such a puce-faced rage that she was able to stand and watch him. It was hard to tell his age. He'd clearly abused his own body but sadly not as much as he had his dog's. The bald thug had bent over and shouted at his bulldog, then punched it in the face.

Did she regret killing him?

Nope.

He had deserved it.

This was when she had had her sandwich business. She had driven around in a van, delivering egg-and-cress and ham-and-cheese to the city's offices. Back then, if you worked in London, the sandwiches came to you. Now, these days, you had to make your own way to the sandwiches and pay six pounds to Pret A Manger for the privilege.

If she had to pinpoint the one change in London since she had been imprisoned that had struck her most, it would have to be Pret A Manger. A business that had not existed before, now occupied every third building. If Pret A Mangers continued to pop up at the same rate it was surely only a matter of time before Prets started to appear on people's bodies, like tumours. Expectant mothers would have their twelve-week scans, only to be told they were gestating a new branch.

When she followed the man out of the park and saw he was headed in the direction of her van, the opportunity was too good not to take. By the time he was beside her vehicle, she'd caught up with him and was able to appeal to him in the way all men of his type could be appealed to. By asking for his expertise.

'Excuse me. I think the refrigerator in my van might be broken. I'm hopeless with that sort of thing. Could you take a look?'

He couldn't resist and within a few seconds he was scratching his head and letting out theatrical sighs as she opened the back doors.

'Let's have a look, shall we?' he had said, clambering into the back, into what was about to become both the worst and the final day of his life.

Carol, standing behind him, had stabbed him in the leg with

her right hand, expertly puncturing his femoral artery. As she had suspected it might, rather than attacking her, his dog had jumped into the van and attacked her sandwiches with gusto. Then she had locked the van doors.

That had been a pleasant few hours for Carol, driving around London, listening to Simon Bates on Radio 1 and the screams of a man bleeding to death while the dog he'd abused enjoyed a delicious feast. You haven't truly heard 'Girls Just Want To Have Fun' until it's been accompanied by the diminishing gurgles of an evil man. Not Simon Bates, of course: the thug in the back of Carol's van.

Once he was dead, she'd got to a payphone and let her customers know she'd have to let them down that day. After a detour to Battersea Dogs & Cats Home, where she dropped off the world's most well-fed rescue dog, she'd treated herself to lunch in an East End café, before heading out to Epping Forest and waiting for the right time to bury the bastard.

A good day. One of her last for some time.

But here she was at Sheldon Oaks, with many more good days in front of her.

Hopefully.

Carol noticed the croquet players heading out to the lawn, like they did most mornings. It occurred to her that she was starting to take these mornings for granted, which was something she couldn't afford to do. People were chasing her, people who thought she'd murdered someone, people who could put her back behind bars. Geoffrey, the ex-detective: what if he got the bit between his teeth and decided to relive his youth, send her down for his One Last Case? He certainly hadn't been backwards in coming forwards when it had come to accusing her in front of everyone the night before.

She had to clear her name, or these few weeks of peace would prove to be nothing but a brief interval from a life spent in prison.

Just her luck to land in a retirement home seemingly entirely populated by criminal investigators. Geoffrey: former detective. Catherine: former forensic pathologist. Margaret: former home secretary. Even Polly, the little old lady who had refused to get into the lift with her: Carol had discovered she was a bestselling crime novelist.

Carol had never understood the appeal of crime fiction. She was like a footballer who didn't watch football. Why spectate when you can take part?

She needed suspects. Suspects and evidence.

The roof. Whoever killed Desmond had access. There was a key. Who had it? Just one key?

That pointed towards staff.

But out on the lawn was a resident who could have wanted Desmond dead. They had the ability and Carol had every reason to believe they had the motive.

She put her arms into her cardigan and slipped on some shoes.

FIFTEEN

The morgue wasn't far from Highgate cemetery. 'Convenient,' said Geoffrey. 'Town planning. You see, there was a time when this country knew what it was doing.'

They took the bus there, which was a novelty for Margaret. Her working life had been all black cabs and ministerial cars. After Parliament, she'd owned a series of VW Golfs she'd been too scared to drive any further than the big Sainsbury's. Thatcher had said that anyone over the age of thirty who found themselves on a bus was a failure. This Margaret wouldn't have put it like that.

It was quite exciting, actually, sitting on a bus, surrounded by people from different walks of life, none of them knowing that she was on her way to her first autopsy.

A younger woman offered Geoffrey her seat but he insisted on not taking it. Silly, really. Watching him sway around on his eighty-year-old legs, out of pride.

One young man was playing music from his phone. No headphones, just out loud, to the whole bus. A kind thought, but Margaret would have appreciated a say in the choice of song. His tune seemed to be mostly about licking a pussy. Didn't pussies lick themselves? I suppose that's one way of giving your cat a bath, thought Margaret.

Margaret was very impressed with the way Catherine directed them to the right place. They were the blue dot on her phone, and as long as the blue dot was going towards the right address, then they were fine. Geoffrey explained that it was all done with satellites and Margaret explained that as a former minister for science, who'd been responsible for funding half of them, she knew that very well.

'Are you sure they're expecting us?' said Margaret. 'All three of us?'

'Don't worry,' said Catherine. 'It's all arranged.'

'And they don't mind us being there?'

'Don't worry.'

They must have been a funny sight, the three of them, shuffling through the car park, looking for the entrance.

A middle-aged man in a crumpled suit was hunched over, working his way through a cigarette. A younger, tidier lady stood beside him, her blonde hair neatly tied back. Margaret recognised them as the police officers who'd come to speak to them in the ballroom the night before.

DCI Bob Beattie stubbed out his cigarette and squinted at the trio of retirees. 'Are you lost?'

'We're looking for the dead bodies,' said Margaret.

'Unless they've moved things around since I worked here, I think we should be fine,' said Catherine. 'Chief Inspector Beattie, yes? And DS Laura ... Sorry, what was it?' Catherine extended her hand.

'Welsh,' said Laura, shaking it.

'Oh, yes. Welsh. You made that terrible joke, didn't you, Bob? What is that? Is it a nerves thing?'

'Sorry, what's going on?' said Bob, agitated.

'My name is Catherine. This is Margaret, and this is Geoffrey. We're residents at Sheldon Oaks and we're here for Desmond's autopsy.'

'Hold up,' said Bob. 'That's not . . . No. I'm sorry, no. That's not going to happen. This isn't a public event.'

'The pathologist is Dr Stephen Turnham, yes? I know Stephen very well. He used to work for me,' said Catherine.

'Okay, but why are you here?' asked Laura. 'Isn't it traditional to wait for the funeral to pay your respects?'

'Well, we're rather worried,' said Catherine. 'There appears to be a murderer on the loose in our home and we think we have something to offer your investigation. I'm a former pathologist. Margaret here is in the House of Lords and used to run the Home Office.'

'And I used to be a copper, which I tried to tell you the other day, but you weren't interested,' said Geoffrey.

Bob let out a sigh, appearing to take a second to adjust to the unusual situation in which he found himself. Flummoxed, he turned to Laura. 'Help me out here, Welsh.'

Laura adopted a professional tone. 'Thank you all for your offers of help. It's clear you have expertise. As I'm sure you can appreciate, a murder investigation is a sensitive thing. We can't allow members of the public, however distinguished, to get involved.'

'Distinguished. Good word, good word,' said Bob. 'Yep.

That's where we're at with it. You're all very distinguished but I'm going to have to ask you, very kindly, to do one.' Bob waggled his thumb, suggesting the direction in which he thought they ought to sod off.

'No, thank you,' said Catherine. 'We're coming in.'

'I don't get it,' said Laura. 'Why do three retired people want to come to an autopsy?'

'Because, my dear,' said Margaret, 'we are *bored*.'

Margaret wasn't sure what to expect. She'd seen this sort of thing on television. Didn't they keep the bodies in drawers? Had she remembered that right? Would the room be cold? She'd dressed for the mild weather, not an indoor freezer. And how would she react when she saw the body? What if she had a completely unexpected response? Fainted or started screaming or broke into uncontrolled song?

The smell hit her. Chemicals, like a photography lab, back when that was still a thing.

'Hello, everybody, hello, Catherine. How exciting. We have an audience today.' The man was in his fifties and carried himself like an accountant. The sort of person, thought Margaret, you'd see on a train eating shortbread biscuits and it would never occur to you that they spent their days with corpses. Beside him there was a plump girl in her twenties. The kind people used to call bubbly. She reminded Margaret of her younger self. 'My name is Dr Stephen Turnham. This is Gemma.'

The echoey room had white brick walls. There was a sink, various pieces of apparatus that hinted at the grim nature of the job: knives, pliers, scissors, a saw. Margaret swallowed. A green hose hung on the wall. Dr Turnham walked over to a table with a black sheet over what Margaret assumed must be the body.

'Is everybody ready?'

They all nodded, solemnly.

'Yes,' said Margaret, quietly. She steadied herself.

Dr Turnham whipped off the sheet to reveal the body of Sir Desmond Crisp, their friend. Margaret instinctively crossed herself. Geoffrey, she noticed, was looking away. He appeared to be going green.

'As you are all aware, he fell from a roughly fifty-foot height,' said Turnham, breezily. 'He appears to have landed on his back. Skull fracture, fractured collar bone, spine broken in five places, broken hip. Trauma to the abdomen resulting in ruptured intestines and a severe leakage of semi-digested beef. Right leg broken. Left leg fine so, for his football career's sake, let's hope he's a left-footer. *Joke*. Severe damage to the brain, heart failure and a collapsed lung. Ladies and gentleman, at this point I can confidently state that this man is dead. But this is where it gets interesting.'

It was about to get *more* interesting? Margaret, fascinated, was already wishing she could relive her life and try pathology as a career.

'Desmond Crisp would most likely have died without the fall. He may have been dead before he came off the roof.'

Bob popped nicotine gum into his mouth and chewed intently.

Dr Turnham pointed to the cadaver's forehead. 'This is a blow to the head, most likely not caused by impact from the fall but by him being struck with an object. You see this circular imprint? It's about forty-five millimetres in diameter. Somebody hit him.'

Catherine quickly took a notepad from her handbag and started scribbling. Laura frowned, annoyed, wondering if she should be doing the same.

The pathologist continued: 'Take a look at the neck. This redness here indicates that the victim was strangled. The abrasions suggest some kind of fabric was in contact with his skin. A scarf could have been used, or perhaps they were wearing gloves.'

'Jesus Christ,' said Bob. 'Some fucker really wanted Des dead.' He then looked to the elderly ladies beside him. 'Excuse my French.'

We're looking at a dead body, thought Margaret. Swear away.

'There's more,' said Dr Turnham. 'We've had a look at his bloods. The victim was poisoned. We're waiting on Toxicology for an exact ID on the substance. Might take a while. Let's just say there're no Speedy Gonzalezes in that department.' He turned to Gemma, his assistant. They rolled their eyes, sharing in a workplace gripe that meant nothing to anyone else in the room.

'All right. Well, thank you, Stephen,' said Catherine, adjusting the shoulder strap on her handbag. 'Is there anything else we should know?'

Bob Beattie looked affronted. He cleared his throat, attempting to establish his control of the room. 'I'll take the lead, if you don't mind. Right. Um. Yeah, is there anything else we should know?'

Dr Turnham thought for a second. 'I can tell you what Desmond Crisp ate for his last meal if you're interested?'

'Ooh, yes, please!' said Margaret.

'Shepherd's pie.'

Margaret's belly rumbled.

The group decided to walk home, across the Heath. Rather a long way, but no one wanted to be the person to say no. They were all shell-shocked by what they'd seen but also, if they were honest with themselves, a little energised.

For London, Hampstead Heath was wild, myriad paths heading in all directions. A lack of order. The taller patches of grass were as high as Margaret.

'Mark my words,' said Geoffrey, focused on nothing but where they'd just been. 'This is the work of an experienced killer.'

'If it was Carol, and I'm not saying it wasn't, but if it was, why Desmond?' said Margaret.

'You don't need a motive,' said Geoffrey. 'Not in a court of law. You just need to be able to prove they did it.'

'Which we can't,' said Catherine. 'I'm with Margaret. Whether it's needed or not, I'd like to know her motive.'

'What we're dealing with is a psychotic mind,' said Geoffrey. 'She did it for the thrill of it.'

Margaret tried to imagine it, the lady she knew murdering – *murdering* – Desmond. 'Well, I thought she was lovely. Perhaps I'm just a terrible judge of character. I suppose the pair of you have psychotic minds too, do you?'

'Is it all right if we take a seat for a moment?' said Catherine.

All three of them fell back onto the same bench, each pensioner making their own unique sound. In the quiet, they heard crickets. A dragonfly fluttered chaotically between blades of grass, entirely unaware that it lived in a city.

'Well, this is nice,' said Margaret.

'Of course, it is one of the most notable gay cruising areas in Europe.'

'Thank you, Geoffrey.'

'Just a little factoid I thought you might find interesting,'

'Yes, thank you, Geoffrey.'

'Personally, I'm all for it. Let people do what they want. Whatever floats your boat. They've got special names for all the things they do, you know.'

'Geoffrey!'

'The spoon! He licked the spoon!' said Catherine.

'Yep, that's one of them—'

'No, at the last baking club. The day before he died. He left early, you remember?'

'Yes, I remember,' said Margaret.

'He asked if he could lick the bowl. He always did that, didn't he? Big kid, really. And Carol—'

Margaret interrupted Catherine with one of her yelps before shouting, 'Carol handed him a spoon!'

SIXTEEN

It was one of those days when clouds passed over quickly. Sun, clouds, sun, clouds. Carol gave Jim a nod and sat beside him on the bench. She could feel the fear her arrival had brought about in the other players. Better to keep a distance. She was looking forward to a time when she didn't terrify nearly everyone she crossed paths with but, for now, she could live without playing croquet. It looked like a stupid game.

'You don't remember me, do you?' said Carol.

'Course I remember you, babe. Been wondering if you was gonna say hello.'

Jim spoke with a wide-boy London accent. Cocky. He was still as handsome as ever, maybe more so. Dressed in a Ralph Lauren cardigan, slacks and moccasins, he looked ready for a yacht. All he was missing was a pipe.

'You could've said hello first.'

'Didn't want you getting a bad rep. Hanging around with the likes of me.'

Deep-voiced and broad-shouldered, Jim had an easy charm. The confidence of a man who was used to being the strongest person in the room. The ladies who hovered around him looked, to Carol, like groupies. Sometimes she got the sense that rather a lot of sex was being had at Sheldon Oaks and that Jim was having most of it. She certainly hadn't had a use for the complimentary condoms she'd found in her bedside drawer.

The gentle breeze sent his fragrance her way. 'That's a nice perfume, Jim,' said Carol.

'It's Antonio Banderas. He's an actor but he makes perfumes on the side. You've to have a back-up in that trade. You gonna join us for a game of croquet? I can teach you the rules, if you like.'

'I think I'll watch if that's all right,' said Carol. 'We can catch up when you're finished.'

Giles jogged through the entrance, presumably returning from a run on the Heath, mud all over his calves. Carol felt like she saw him running every day. Always either running or on edge, stressing about something. Those were the only two things that those sort of men ever did: jog and stress.

She closed her eyes. The gentle knocking sound of mallets hitting balls was oddly tranquillising. That's what had been missing. Noise. It was so quiet here. Prison was a noisy place. Creaking pipes, slamming doors, the constant yells of inmates.

Something occurred to her and her eyes snapped open. Her eyesight wasn't what it used to be, but, from where she was, she could just about see that Tyler was hammering with his right hand.

'I thought you'd retired.' Jim sat next to her on the bench. He waved goodbye to his friends. 'See you tomorrow.'

'I have,' said Carol. 'Did you win?'

'It's not really a winning game the way we play it. Just knocking some balls about.' He touched her knee with his. 'Everyone thinks you did Crisp.'

'I don't kill any more. Do you?'

'Not in a *loooong* time, babes. I like croquet now.'

Carol thought back to the first time they'd met, in Epping Forest. 'Did I ever thank you?'

'Didn't need to. I was only doing what any gentleman who was raised right would do. Can't let a lady dig a hole on her own. I never asked you. Why d'you kill that bloke?'

'He kicked a dog.'

Jim looked straight ahead and nodded his approval. 'Too right.'

'What about yours?' asked Carol.

'What, *that* body? On that day? Don't remember.'

'Do you miss it?' asked Carol.

'What? Murder? No. See, that's why you and me was different. It was only ever a part of the job for me. I'd've never killed anyone if I didn't have to. You do it for the love.'

'*Did* it.'

Jim smiled. 'If you say so. And if you did do Des, I don't care. This place is full of busies. I'm not getting involved.'

'You might have to be.'

'Oh, yeah?'

'Or maybe you already are.'

'Spit it out, babes.'

Time for Carol to admit that she hadn't come to watch the croquet. 'I heard you had a big row with Desmond. What was that about?'

'Suspect, am I?'

'They're all after me. If I don't find the killer, I'll be back in Bronzefield by the end of the week.'

'Wouldn't be so bad, would it? Women's prison always looked like fun to me. All netball and knitting. You wanna try Wandsworth.'

'I'm done with it, Jim. I've just discovered Americanos. There's a sauna here, karaoke night . . . I had a butternut squash risotto for dinner last night. A butternut squash risotto, Jim! Went into the village, found a nice little restaurant, looked at the menu and ordered myself a butternut squash risotto.'

'How was it?'

'All right. Should have had the chicken, but the point is that I *could*. I'm not going back. So, this fight with Desmond. What was it about?'

Jim looked into the middle distance. 'Old stuff.'

'What old stuff? You did a stretch, didn't you? He the one who caught you?'

'No. Wouldn't care if he did. That was his job. Cops and robbers, innit? Nah, this was about a debt he never paid.'

'What debt?' Carol was enjoying her new role of interrogator.

'I can't be telling you that. That was business between me and him. It gets out and I'm dead too. You're all right, I trust you, babes, but I can't risk it.'

Huh. Carol sat there, pondering the situation. She knew Jim wouldn't budge. No point trying. She'd have to find out the truth another way.

'I guess I'll just have to ask you where you were when he died, then.'

'What time did he die then? I ain't got a clue.'

'Three fifteen p.m.'

'Three fifteen p.m., Friday.' Jim searched his mind. 'Oh. Easy. I'd have been in my place, watching *Escape to the Country*.'

'Anyone who can verify that for you?'

'Sorry, love. It was a good one. Surrey couple, I think. Looking for a property in Scotland.'

'Did they buy anything?'

'Nope. They never fucking do.'

And with that, Jim got up and headed back towards the building, swinging his croquet mallet in his left hand.

SEVENTEEN

Margaret and Catherine stared at Geoffrey. They were on the bistro patio, sharing a pot of tea. No one had been allowed to say anything for what felt like an age. The place was in its post-lunch lull, not many residents around. Margaret had managed to persuade a waiter to sell her an Eccles cake, even though the kitchen was closed. A playlist of generic jazz played so quietly as to be hardly noticeable.

'Are you trying to work out—'

Geoffrey held up his hand and scrunched his eyes. 'Quiet, Margaret. Please. Sorry, I'm trying to think.'

'Twenty-seven hours,' whispered Catherine. 'He's trying to work out the time between Desmond licking Carol's spoon and Desmond dying. It's twenty-seven hours.'

Margaret nodded her understanding and they both continued to sit in silence until Geoffrey slammed the table with his hand in satisfaction.

'Twenty-seven hours!' he said. 'That's how long there was between Desmond licking the spoon and Desmond dying. Twenty-seven hours.'

Margaret and Catherine politely raised their eyebrows as if this were new information.

'Catherine, this is your area,' said Geoffrey. 'I'm thinking slow-acting poison. Thoughts?'

Catherine paused, happy for the opportunity to engage her brain. All of the information was still there. She just hadn't used it for a long time. It didn't take long to come to her.

'Thallium,' she said. 'Thallium sulphate. It's slow-acting, odourless, colourless ... lovely poison. If that's what you're looking for. Mind you, it's really *very* slow-acting. Can take as long as a month to do the job.'

'Ah, but there you go, you see.' Geoffrey raised a finger, making his point. 'That's why she ended up hitting him on the head, throwing him off the roof. It was taking too long.'

Catherine frowned.

'What?' said Margaret.

'I don't think it's easy to get hold of,' said Catherine. 'Not a big enough dose to kill anyone.'

'But like Geoffrey says,' pondered Margaret, 'maybe she didn't have a big enough dose. That's why she did all the other stuff, the strangling, the bludgeoning and the pushing.'

Catherine and Geoffrey shared a look.

'Doesn't make sense, does it?' said Geoffrey.

'No, it doesn't,' said Catherine.

'What?' said Margaret.

'She's a seasoned killer,' said Geoffrey. 'Doesn't that strike you as rather ...'

Catherine finished his sentence: '... amateur. Surely she knows enough about poison to get it right first time?'

Margaret slurped her tea, then spoke: 'So Carol didn't do it?'

'Oh, she did it,' said Geoffrey. 'I'm sure of it. Just not sure we've got all the pieces in the right places yet.'

Catherine fiddled with her phone. Margaret thought about heading back up to her apartment. This new purpose they had was welcome but it didn't mean she was entirely abandoning the leisurely pace she'd grown used to living at. Would a biscuit with the cup of tea she'd have in front of *Bargain Hunt* be greedy? Considering the Eccles cake she'd just had? No one else need know about it, but wasn't that worse? Like a drinker who hid bottles of vodka under the bed.

'Ha!' said Catherine, with satisfaction.

'What?' said Margaret.

'Look! Carol Quinn's CV.' Catherine held up her phone. 'It's on LinkedIn, that horrible website they all use for their careers now.'

'Oh, it's ghastly,' said Margaret.

'Oh, yes, totally ghastly,' said Geoffrey, trying to give the impression that he knew what they were talking about.

'They must have made her do it in prison, as part of her rehabilitation,' said Catherine. 'But look, right here, look! She used to work in a laboratory.'

Margaret took Catherine's phone and held it close to her face, squinting. 'Oh, my, you're right. At St Thomas's, yes. Only as a receptionist, though.'

Geoffrey took his turn to squint at the phone. 'Excellent work, Catherine. This is damning. *Damning.*'

Margaret was sceptical. 'Really? It was nearly fifty years ago!'

'Yes, but ...' The new find had injected Geoffrey with

energy. He stood up and paced. 'If she's worked in a lab, we have very good reason to believe she has connections, knowledge, *access to poison.*'

'I suppose it's *possible*,' said Margaret, not wishing to pooh-pooh a man in his stride.

Geoffrey held up the phone. 'I think we need to take this to the police.'

EIGHTEEN

As Carol was returning to the building after her conversation with Jim, Hannah Newsom and her husband, Shep, arrived at Sheldon Oaks in a newly purchased Range Rover. They were there to pick up some of Hannah's father's things. They parked out front, not far from the exact same spot, Carol noted, where Hannah's father's skull had cracked open a couple of days earlier.

Desmond had introduced them to her a week or two ago in the bistro. Hannah and Shep were about forty and Carol had taken an instant dislike to the pair of them. She'd politely turned down their offer of joining them and instead sat at a table nearby, pretended to read, and listened to every word of their conversation.

Hannah did that thing where she never laughed, but instead simply stated that something was funny. So her dad would make a joke and she would say, 'That's hilarious' or 'That's just so, like, funny to me?' with a completely straight face.

Hannah and Shep had private-school accents – only a man born into the elite could get away with having a dog's name, thought Carol. Despite their plummy voices, the pair talked in a kind of Californian business-speak. When Desmond had realised that the table didn't have any packets of sugar, Shep, instead of saying, 'I'll get some,' had said, 'Let me see if I can action that for you.' When Desmond had pointed out that the flowers were starting to bloom, instead of saying, 'Oh, that's nice,' Hannah had said, 'That's so empowering.'

The topic of conversation had been the cost of living. The kids' school fees had just gone up and Shep, he said, was having cash-flow problems. By Q3 next year (whatever that was) he was expecting to be 'generating maximum ROI' but right now his business was in a 'transitional phase'. The business, as far as Carol could tell, was a podcast that hadn't yet released an episode, in which Shep gave business advice.

'I wouldn't expect you to understand everything, Des, but I'm going to be passing on all of my own acquired expertise, invaluable advice, you know – dress for the job you want, protein not carbs, time management, you know. This is the sort of stuff you're not going to be able to get on any other business podcast. Peter Wires, he's one of the big business gurus out there right now, he suggests that, if you want to get anywhere as a CEO, you need to be waking up at four a.m. My USP – which stands for Ultra Selling Potential, by the way, Des – is that I'm going to suggest that people get up at three. Peter Wires is not going to know what's hit him.'

'It's really great stuff, Dad,' Hannah had said. 'Whole thing's a no-brainer.'

'It's the kind of thing people are going to be willing to pay for. It *will* make money, I've got no doubt about that, but in order to reach an audience I need a marketing budget, and you know this, Des – cash is king, you know.'

'And I suppose you want mine.'

'You're so funny, Dad,' Hannah had said.

Carol had no idea if Desmond had given them the money they had asked for, but it was fair to say he hadn't looked especially keen in the bistro that day.

Carol watched the couple chatting by their car. Today wasn't a day for eavesdropping. If she was going to truly investigate, she'd have to ask some questions. Carol gingerly approached them, giving the friendliest little wave she could muster.

'Hello, I'm Carol. We met the other day. I'm very sorry for your loss.'

'That's so sweet of you to say.' Hannah had her arms outstretched. 'Are you a hugger? Because I'm a hugger.'

'I'm not a hugger, but thank you,' said Carol.

'Baby, you can't leave the dogs in the car.'

'Well, we can't bring them in there, can we?' said Shep.

'You stay out here with them. I'll go in.'

Hannah gave her two cockerpoos slobbery kisses and put on, nonsensically, Carol thought, a pair of big dark Prada sunglasses just as she was heading indoors. Since Carol had last seen her, Hannah looked like she'd gained a kilo or two and a couple of million pounds.

Carol and Shep were left alone together with the two dogs. She looked down at her feet, Shep held the leads. An odd moment, less than a second, but she felt it. *Am I really staying here with him?* Having shared a cell, for six years, with an awful woman called Brenda, Carol was not the type to spend any longer with a person she didn't like than was entirely necessary. But her future depended on finding out the truth. She had to extract as much information as she could.

'Nice car. Is it new?'

'Yes. Purchased this week.' Shep used the most irritating pronunciation available, putting the emphasis in 'purchased' on 'chased'.

'Podcast doing well, then?'

Shep looked blank for a second. *Podcast?* 'Oh, yes, the, uh, the podcast. Yes, it's going terrifically, thank you.'

'I'm afraid I'm a little behind on all the podcasts. I'm not sure I've ever heard one. I keep reading about it. They have a Podcast of the Week in the paper but they never explain where we're supposed to get it from. It's a computer thing, isn't it?'

Carol knew exactly what a podcast was. She was addicted to the true-crime ones and was a little insulted no one had yet made one about her. She decided that, with Shep, the best way of prying without arousing suspicion was to play the role of 'doddery old lady'.

'I'm not as bad with computers as some of the folk here. Margaret – I don't know if you know her? She prints out her emails just to read them. Now that's silly, isn't it?'

'I don't know. Not necessarily. Mark Zuckerberg has his emails read to him every morning while he's in his flotation tank.'

'Is that right? He a friend of yours, is he?'

'He's a businessman. Started Facebook?'

'Oh, yes, I'm on that. Total nonsense. People talk such rubbish, don't they? So, your podcast? Where can I listen to it? Will I be able to get it on cassette?'

'It's not out yet, actually, just working towards optimisation, you know.'

'Aren't we all?'

Carol wanted to ask a very personal question. She thought she knew the answer but she wanted to be sure. She decided that rather than trying to disguise the intrusiveness of the question the best thing to do was to underline it. Make a joke of it. You could, at her age, get away with a lot. Old women were just nosy. That was the stereotype. Why not exploit it?

'So, new car. You've come into some money, haven't you? Forgive me, I'm just an old gossip. Was Hannah left a lot in the will?'

Shep laughed, giddy. You got the sense he was delighted at the chance to talk about it. He lowered his voice. '*Millions.*'

'Oh, isn't that lovely? Shame it had to come in such tragic circumstances.'

Shep tried and failed to remove the smile from his face. 'Yes, tragic. Very very tragic. Gone too soon. May he rest in peace. Giles!'

Giles, out of his running clothes now, was passing by.

'Shep! Buddy!'

The two men went into an enthusiastic embrace. Shep immediately looked at ease now that someone his own age was there. Someone of his own background. Carol was all too aware of the effect her age could have on some younger people. It made them uncomfortable. Oh, yeah, sure, you've lived a long life. Well done and all that. But how does one *talk* to that? Too many people just didn't know.

'I suppose this is the last we'll be seeing of you,' said Giles.

'Oh, you haven't seen the last of me, G-Man. I've still got some pitches I want to run up your flagpole. There's so much you're not doing with this place that you could. Here's two words for you. Ice. Rink.'

Carol, despite her mission, found herself edging away. It was the phrase 'G-Man'. Shep, it had to be said, was not her sort of person. Luckily for him, that was no longer an executable offence. She found herself in a daydream, picturing Shep's face going through all the colours of the rainbow, as she squeezed his throat until the life fell out of him. One more kill? For old times' sake?

'Well, I'll be off, then. Lovely to see you both,' she said, with a jolly smile.

They said their goodbyes and as she entered the building the conversation continued.

'Okay, okay, no ice rink. What if you apply for a licence for a euthanasia clinic? They do it here, on site, you get a cut of the fee.'

'Only problem with that, mate, we'd be killing all our customers.'

'Right, right, yeah, see what you're getting at, buddy. See what you're getting at.'

'Actually, buddy,' said Giles, 'there is something I needed to talk to you about . . .'

Their voices blessedly drifted away as the automatic doors closed behind her. Carol had no desire to hear whatever inane direction the two men's conversation was headed in. She approached the front desk. Before she went back to her apartment, she wanted to check something. Derek, the security guard, was asleep in his chair. So sedentary was he that he reminded her of a pet you constantly found yourself checking wasn't dead. By contrast, the always-on-her-feet Elisa was by the lifts, in an animated conversation with Tyler.

Carol focused. In a hurry, she opened up the guest book and went straight to Friday, the day of Desmond's murder.

Yes. He was there: 3 p.m.

Shep Newsom.

Fifteen minutes before the murder.

Shep Newsom.

The murder that had made him a millionaire.

Shep Newsom.

NINETEEN

Carol sat at the desk pushed up against the wall in her living room, poured herself a Bacardi and Coke and switched on her computer. She already knew what her first search would be: shep newsom companies house. Carol took pride in how confident she was with computers for a woman her age. In prison, in preparation for her return to civilised society, she'd been made to go through a series of courses, turning her into a productive citizen. This amounted to learning how to make a CV and putting it on LinkedIn. Carol pictured prospective employers looking at the seventy-five-year-old lady in front of them: 'There's a thirty-five-year gap on your CV. Can you explain that for me?'

'Oh, that? Funny story, actually.'

When fiddling around in the prison computer room, she'd discovered Companies House as a fun place to snoop on people online. Any company who'd ever been registered with HMRC was on there and you could take a look at their basic accounts. Shep Newsom got no results. She searched Shep Newsom on Google. Can't be many Shep Newsoms can there? Only one, in fact, had made any kind of impact on the internet. Her Shep Newsom, most likely the only Shep Newsom to have ever lived.

But that couldn't be his real name, could it? The upper classes, as mad as they were, were not bonkers enough to name a human 'Shep' surely. Carol had had minimal contact with the very upper echelons of society, but she wasn't completely ignorant of their ways. Every now and then a wayward society girl with a coke habit would pass through the prison service. They all had ridiculous nicknames – Filly, Tilly, Scratch, Muffin, Piggy. Shep had to be a nickname. She scrolled through his Facebook page. Not much action in recent years, but there were some old posts. One picture he'd been tagged in by someone else caught her eye. He was sixteen, maybe? In some Edwardian-looking school uniform, his head bent back in entitled arrogance. Big, curly, centre-parted hair. Well, that explained the nickname. He looked like a dog. Looking through the comments, one caught her attention: 'That's my Dom.'

Dominic Henry Maximilian Newsom, she discovered, had been the director of forty-something companies in his time, all of which had apparently collapsed.

The snowboarding business: dissolved. The tuna jerky business: dissolved. Six different microbreweries (what was it with talentless public-school boys and microbreweries?): all dissolved.

Shep was a man with a large online presence, a record of failure. Various websites and YouTube videos with thirty views suggested he'd tried his hand at everything. He had, for a month, attempted being a left-wing talking head, opining on why baking shows were a tool of Western imperialism. Then, when that hadn't worked, he'd switched to being a right-wing head-banger, yelling about how Britain's rainy climate was the fault of Muslims. That had, to be fair, earned him a brief stint as a GB News contributor.

The overall picture was of a man who desperately wanted to be seen as a success, in direct contrast to his actual ability to become one. At one stage, he had set up an online course in which he taught midwifery. Five hundred pounds for six weeks. No takers. Well, now he had money. Carol figured that with a track record like his it wouldn't last long. She dreaded to think of the plans he had for it: a fashion label? An action movie? His own nuclear power station?

So, she had a clear motive. Shep and Hannah had stood to gain from Desmond's death and they had already done so. The money surely hadn't come through yet but they had certainly started spending it. Shep had also been in the building when Desmond had died. But how had Shep got onto the roof?

Another question: if the inheritance was theirs, why hadn't they just waited for Desmond to die? He was eighty. It might not have arrived as quickly as they would have wanted but it was surely in the post. Des was a fit-looking eighty-year-old, though. Perhaps they couldn't wait. Carol could only imagine the debts a man like Shep would have accumulated.

Carol's sofa was calling her. Dinnertime was approaching but she didn't feel like eating. Her own sigh surprised her. Was this depression? She was certainly glum. She felt she'd made a couple of breakthroughs in the case – the left-handed theory, the will recipients – but she had no one to share them with. Margaret, Catherine, even Geoffrey, she genuinely liked them. As a younger woman she'd allowed herself to be consumed by disappointment with the people the world was offering up. Yes, she'd eliminated some of the worst examples, but then she'd gone to prison, a place where terrible people seemed to seep out of the walls. In those three, she thought she'd found her first chance for real friends since school. She thought herself a good judge of character and theirs, to her, seemed true. They offered her the chance to be a normal person, doing normal things, which only now did she realise was something she wanted to try on for size.

Her computer had gone into sleep mode and she wasn't far off herself.

Maybe this was it. She was destined never to have friends. They all thought she'd killed someone, and they were all investigators, trusted members of society. Maybe Shep did it, maybe Jim, maybe Tyler, maybe Giles, maybe Elisa or Belinda or Polly for all she knew, but Carol was a convicted serial killer, for Heaven's sake. People's minds were sure to settle on her. What chance did she have swimming against that tide?

In recent days she'd found herself visualising murder again. In the first person. She recognised that itch and she knew how to scratch it. Was she really thinking about returning to the field of play?

If she was headed back to prison anyway, why not do what she was good at one last time? Do what you love. There is no greater tragedy than a wasted talent. Why rob the world of her gift? Killing was what Carol Quinn was good at. A victim wouldn't be hard to find. She was in a city of ten million. The deserving were everywhere.

A fork in the road. Investigate? Or add to the total?

Maybe she could do both.

She was still. In an old but familiar reverie.

Yes, Carol would kill again.

She jumped. A knock at the door. She stood up to answer it, her fists still clenched, nails digging into her palms.

TWENTY

'Hi, Carol.' Elisa, standing at Carol's door with a smile.

'Hello, Elisa.' Carol wondered if her face betrayed the violent fantasies she'd just been going through in her head.

'I just thought I'd check in to see if you were joining us in the ballroom this evening?'

'The ballroom?'

'Yes, perhaps you've seen the posters? We've hired some entertainment for you all.'

Ah, yes. The Vera Lynn Tribute Act. Britain hadn't quite yet caught up with the age of its pensioners. Carol and many of the other residents were younger than Paul McCartney and yet much of the country still saw old people as Second World War veterans. She had, in fact, heard Tyler ask Geoffrey the other day if he'd fought in the Battle of the Somme. Geoffrey had had to explain that that would make him something like 130 years old to which Tyler had responded, 'Oh, right, and you're younger than that, yeah?' Geoffrey hadn't been offended and had taken the opportunity to go into a twenty-minute lecture on why the First World War had started, as Tyler picked up a mallet and banged in a new fence post, not listening to a word.

'Oh, yes, the entertainment,' said Carol. 'I'm a little tired, I'll see how I feel.'

'Well, I do hope you manage to make it. I've noticed you looking a little down these last few days. I know some fingers have been pointed at you.' Elisa put a hand on Carol's shoulder. 'It must be difficult for you.'

'Thank you, Elisa. I'm sure I'll pop down for a bit.'

It was as if Carol had stepped back fifty years and entered one of the bars from her youth. Only everyone was now older, greyer, and some of the men's heads were swollen from decades of booze. But that energy was there. The feeling that anything might happen. Given her new resolution to kill again, truly, it might.

She scoped the room for potential victims.

Polly, the crime writer, sat in a chair knitting, a blanket over her lap. Already nearly at death's door. All she needed was a nudge. If Carol could somehow get into her bedroom she could ease her into the afterlife with a pillow over the face. Instead of a kebab on the way home, Carol could treat herself to a murder. But what would be the point? When it came to murder, Carol was one of the greats. Why do something an amateur could? Only the deserving. That had been her general rule. Carol wasn't about to start murdering harmless old ladies.

Geoffrey. Get him alone and she was sure she could stab him. She could picture it now, the blade entering and re-entering his chest, while he explained to her that going through his rib cage was expending too much energy and that she would, in fact, be far more efficient if she went for his neck or abdomen.

Giles was standing at the side of the room, observing. He was always pensive but what about? Getting caught? Who's to say Giles didn't murder Desmond? Killing the killer would be a nice touch. She could give him something to really worry about. Lock him in his office and pump it full of gas? Get herself on the roof and take sniper shots at him while he jogged on the Heath? Impractical, no doubt, but the fantasy was pleasant.

Jim. Now, that would present a challenge. She'd be going up against an ex-pro from the men's game. He deserved a proper ending. Still months until fireworks night, she thought. Let a couple of boxes of rockets off in his bed. Would that do the trick? He was certainly the sort of man to appreciate that kind of creativity. Far-fetched, though, jumping the shark. Was Carol losing her knack for the subtle kill? There was beauty in that.

But the mood in the bar tonight was happy. Killing would make her such a party pooper, and if there was one thing worse than a serial killer, it was a party pooper.

Carol sat at the bar with her Bacardi and Coke, girlishly playing with her straw. Chairs and tables had been moved to the side, leaving an empty makeshift dance-floor in the centre of the room. Would the evening end with the boys and girls pairing up for a slow dance? There would be no chaperones. Things could get rude.

She spotted Belinda, who, having made such a show when the police had spoken to everyone, now appeared to have moved on to the stage of grief in which you sat on the lap of your new, much younger boyfriend. Belinda tossed her hair around like an armless woman with nits. Carol knew her type. A woman who had defined herself by the effect she had on men, desperately clinging to her powers. Fair enough, but what had that display in the hall been about?

I cannot be the murderer because I loved Desmond and he loved me.

Perhaps it was true, but why announce it like that? It was, to Carol, a little suspicious, a case of protesting rather too much. And if it were true, Belinda's capacity for moving on was impressive. Who was that young man Belinda was now whispering tenderly to? He was out of uniform but he looked to Carol awfully like one of the restaurant's waiters. Yes, it was Marco, the handsome Italian. A staff member. Now there was someone who might have access to a key to the roof.

The Vera Lynn act looked to be a drama graduate with the skills to pay *some* of the bills. Not all. Some.

'It's been such a pleasure to sing to you all this evening. I hope I brought back some memories. I can see you all now, in the Underground stations, 'aving a li'le sing-song. Well, here's a number that should bring it all back.'

'We'll Meet Again' started up for the fourth time. I went to see David Bowie, thought Carol.

Some in the room enthusiastically sang along, waving their arms in the air. Carol had noticed among her generation, the 'boomers', a large contingent who seemed to believe that, although they hadn't been born until after 1945, they had personally won the Second World War.

'Not your kind of music?' Elisa asked Carol, sidling up beside her at the bar.

'Not really, no. I'm having a good time, though.'

'Good. That makes me happy.' Elisa worked her way around the room, smiling at each table, finally stopping next to Belinda and her beau for a chat.

Once fake Vera Lynn had finished, Giles took to the stage. 'Wasn't that fantastic? And such a reasonable rate! All right, ladies and gentlemen, the evening does not finish there. The bar is still open, so do get yourselves refreshed.' Tyler was now making his way to a sound board on the stage, out of his overalls and in a horrifically bright jumper, which seemed to signify his new night-time persona. 'DJ Tyler has agreed to keep up the entertainment by running a little karaoke so, if you think you can sing, get your name down! Isn't this a fantastic place to live?'

There was a smattering of applause and a rush for the bar. Giles continued: 'Don't forget, if you have friends who you think would enjoy living here, please put them in touch. We do offer discounted deals for friends of Sheldon Oaks so don't be shy. Have a lovely evening!'

The first singer, as Carol had heard was always the case, was Jim. He confidently launched into 'Mack The Knife'. Square-jawed, with a nice-fitting suit, the man had charisma. All those years ago, when Carol had met him, he'd had blood down his shirt, but the same easy charm. Carol looked around the room. Some of the ladies staring at Jim had Beatlemania in their eyes. With Desmond gone, there was no doubting who Top Dog was now. Jim was the home's alpha.

'Bitch!' Carol turned. It was Belinda, standing over her, furious. Before Carol had a second to think, Belinda threw her glass of wine into her face. Carol caught a taste. Pinot Grigio. Belinda really did have no class at all.

'What the fuck are you talking about, Belinda?'

This had come out of nowhere. Violence was in the air but, like riding a bike, you never forget. This was Carol's comfort zone.

'You called me a slut.'

Carol had no idea what she was talking about but the situation was enough for a switch to flick. This was it. Back in business. Time to remount the horse named Murder.

Carol took the small bottle of Coke on the bar, flipped it over and smashed it. In no time at all she had created a weapon good enough to do the job. She, Carol Quinn, elderly woman and subscriber to *Puzzles Weekly* magazine, was holding the jagged edge of a broken bottle at the throat of another old lady. Before Carol had a chance to ram it into the side of Belinda's neck, into Belinda's carotid artery, before the blood began to spurt out, pretty, like a fountain, she felt a hand grab her arm and heard a voice she'd heard before.

DCI Bob Beattie.

'That's enough of that. Carol Quinn, I'm arresting you on suspicion of the murder of Sir Desmond Crisp.'

TWENTY-ONE

Vending-machine coffee in a plastic cup brought back memories. Bad ones. Carol should have been in bed, falling asleep to *Women Who Kill*. Instead she was sitting on a ledge, listening to the mindless yells of the shoplifting junkie in the neighbouring police cell. They all sounded the same. For years, the moans, groans and ramblings of addicts had been her birdsong.

At least this time she'd been able to entertain herself with her phone. That was one advantage of being the age she was. The desk sergeant had taken pity on her and allowed her to keep her mobile. She'd sat there, scrolling through Facebook, looking at old friends still in prison. Perhaps she'd be seeing them again soon.

She saw herself in that moment, holding the bottle to Belinda's throat. That had been her opportunity but she hadn't taken it. There had been enough time, but she'd paused. Carol was no longer a woman who killed. She was like Mike Tyson at the end of his career. The murderous rage had left her and it would never return. That afternoon, she'd thought it was back but it wasn't. That was just an echo. That was just, in truth, a sadness. But she was no longer a woman who expressed her feelings through the medium of killing. She needed a new hobby.

The irony was not lost on her. On the evening she'd learnt, definitively, that she could no longer kill, when she'd had it confirmed that she did not have it in her . . . she'd been arrested for murder. Funny old game.

A judder rising up from her chest caught Carol by surprise and then . . . Was she? She was. She was crying. Carol hadn't cried this century. Prison hadn't allowed it. The shell she had grown for herself hadn't allowed it. Carol had retired her tear ducts at an early age. They had had as much use as her appendix. Crying was a weakness she could not afford yet here she was, alone, in a police cell, blubbering like a little girl.

Carol did not want to go back to prison.

She found herself overwhelmed by all the forgotten feelings of crying. The shame and embarrassment, then the relief. She embraced the release and began to wail. It felt good. Decades of tension leaving her body. Carol was expressing her feelings without murdering. Emotion without a death count. Was this what her prison counsellor had called personal growth?

But prison was not a world in which she could do this, where *this* Carol could survive. She had to fight to stay on the outside. She had a life left to live.

The shutter on her cell door slid open and Laura Welsh's face appeared.

'All right, Carol. We're ready for you now.'

Carol wiped her eyes with her sleeve and composed herself.

TWENTY-TWO

Even after hearing about her crimes, Catherine had struggled to picture Carol as the killer. But after seeing her attack Belinda, she knew it had to be true.

Catherine had spent much of the previous day considering how Carol had gone about poisoning Desmond. Having Desmond lick the bowl had been a clever trick but how had she, so expertly, managed not to contaminate the rest of the cake mixture? They'd all eaten the results. They hadn't tasted good but, and perhaps this was the kindest thing you could say about the cakes Margaret and Carol had made last Friday, they hadn't been poisoned.

Catherine stopped swimming and took a rest, hanging at the edge of the Ladies Pond on Hampstead Heath. The sun was just coming up. The air was as fresh as it got in North London, which was not especially fresh but fresh enough. Fresh enough for Catherine.

She'd spent a career analysing death. In the case of murder, her remit had been 'what' and 'how', rather than 'who'. 'Who' was exciting. She'd been enjoying 'who' and now she wanted to know 'why'.

Well, the police had Carol now. A fun little interlude but the case was closed. Catherine would probably never see Carol again, probably never find out 'why'. Perhaps she'd visit her in prison and get the full story. That could be a day trip to look forward to. What if Carol agreed to her visit, but only under the condition that Catherine smuggled in a condom stuffed with drugs up her rectum? Something to consider.

Pushed, strangled, bludgeoned, poisoned – what a thorough job she'd done on poor Desmond! There was a lot to admire about Carol. Not many women of her age had that kind of vim. Catherine worked hard at her fitness, all those nuts and berries, overnight oats, morning swims and evening Pilates. But if she really wanted to, would she have the energy for all of *that*?

Catherine blushed. Last night, after the excitement of Carol's arrest, she'd had a slow dance with Geoffrey. It was the closest her body had been to a man's since Nigel had left. To her surprise, she'd found herself rather liking it. That was until Geoffrey had started talking. The song had been 'Imagine' by John Lennon, and Geoffrey had been unable to resist explaining to Catherine that if you had a world without countries and possessions, then they would have to be created because human nature required them. 'What Lennon is doing here is selling anarchy as Utopia and I'm afraid I just can't sign up to that, Catherine.' It had been a shame because, until he'd started talking, Catherine had, in that moment, found herself rather attracted to Geoffrey. Companionship, human contact – they could be nice things to have. If she could just stop the man opening his mouth. Perhaps she'd wait until

Geoffrey showed signs of dementia and seduce him when he became mute.

Catherine squinted at what she thought was the rising sun but soon came to realise was, in fact, just the palest body she'd ever seen. It was Geoffrey, in nothing but boxers, walking around the side of the pond towards her.

'Don't mind me, I'm just here for a swim,' he shouted as he moved, to no one in particular. 'Ah, Catherine, I knew you'd be here, and I had to speak to you. Excuse my current state. This was the only way I could think of being inconspicuous.'

'Good morning, Geoffrey. This is the Ladies' Pond.'

'Catherine, I've been up all night thinking.'

Dear God, was this about to be a declaration of love?

'The police have Carol but I'm worried that the case will go on for ever, because they always do and I may not last all that long and I'll never find out why she did it. Catherine, I have to know why she did it. I can't stop our investigation.'

'I've been thinking the same thing,' said Catherine, trying to look at Geoffrey's face and not his body.

'I remembered something. I have a key to Desmond's apartment. He had a key to mine. It was a little arrangement in case we locked ourselves out. Pointless, really, seeing as the front desk have keys to all our places, but I've always done it with a neighbour, just out of habit, you know.'

'Geoffrey, perhaps you might like to get to the point. You're shivering and I think that lifeguard might be heading straight for you.'

'Catherine, I think we need to take a look inside Desmond's apartment. There may be some evidence there.'

'Give me five minutes to get changed.'

Catherine remembered something and shouted at Geoffrey's naked hairy back as he walked away with purpose. 'Geoffrey!'

'Yes.'

'Me and Carol had the same arrangement.'

'Oh, yes?'

'I have a key to her place too.'

TWENTY-THREE

DS Laura Welsh and DCI Bob Beattie walked and talked along one of the many dull corridors in Hampstead police station. On the floor, every few feet, were mousetraps. Not Laura's job to deal with, thankfully.

'Can I lead this one?' she asked Bob.

'Not this one, sorry. Next time.'

Laura stopped moving.

Bob played dumb. 'What?'

'It's twenty-four degrees outside, Bob. Does that sound like January weather to you?'

'No.'

'Leaves? On the trees? You noticed they're back, Bob? Does that look like January weather to you?'

'Laura.'

'After Christmas. That's when you said I could lead an interview. It's June.'

'June not after Christmas? I'd say it's well after Christmas. True to my word.'

Laura stared at him. She wasn't in the mood to be fobbed off with joviality. Bob clocked on. 'Sorry. I should have let you do one. But this one, there's too many factors at play.'

'Oh, yeah. Factors. Are you going to let me in on all those factors or what? I've read the file on Desmond. Investigated for corruption and cleared of all charges, but that's not the whole story, is it? He was the boss. They were never going to do him.'

'I'm just worried about where this might lead,' said Bob. 'I don't want you going down alleyways that ain't gonna help us. There's shit we want to avoid. Trust me.'

'I don't trust you, Bob. You said after Christmas. It's June. *June*. You're just a big boys' club, aren't you?'

Bob looked at his shoes, then up at Laura. Then, seeing the strength of her stare, he turned back to his shoes. 'Look. This should be a pretty simple case. We've got a killer in there. I know she did it. You know she did it. I just don't want us causing ourselves unnecessary bother.'

'If it's a pretty simple case then let me do it. I've done the reading. She confessed to everything last time around. If she did it, which, like you say, we know she did, we'll be done in ten.'

Bob relented and stretched out his arm, gesturing for Laura to lead the way. She took a deep breath and walked in.

A table in a cold grey room, with Carol sitting on one side, Laura and Bob on the other. Carol took a sip of her coffee, in a chipped cup this time, and waited.

'Okay. I have a few questions I need to get through before we start,' said Laura, looking down at her checklist. 'How is your mental health today?'

Carol frowned. 'Fine.'

'Do you have any allergies?'

'No.'

'And are there any subjects you find triggering?'

'I beg your pardon?'

'Are there any topics which, if brought up, are liable to cause you distress?'

'Murder.'

'Sorry?'

'Yes, murder, violence, conflict in general, really. So, if we could stay away from those areas, I'd appreciate it.'

'Right. Um . . .'

Laura looked down at her notes and underlined nothing in particular.

Stalling for time, thought Carol.

'She's pissing you about,' said DCI Bob Beattie, sticking a nicotine patch onto his arm. 'Aren't you, Carol? You know the score.'

'It's a long time since I've been in an interrogation room.' Carol leant back and sighed.

'Yeah, I'd imagine it is,' said Bob. 'What was it, thirty, forty years ago?'

'Split the difference.'

'I wasn't even on the force then.'

'Not much has changed,' said Carol. 'The icebreaker questions are new. Do you want to go ahead and ask me the big one, DCI Beattie?'

'I'm asking the questions,' said Laura, making a point of taking control.

'Oh, I'm sorry. Good. Go ahead, dear.' Carol returned to her coffee. It was going cold.

Laura looked her in the eye. 'Did you kill Desmond Crisp?'

Bob winced.

'No. Can I go home now or do you have any more questions?'

Laura looked down at her notepad. 'Right, but you are a killer, yes?'

'I have killed. You've both read my files by now, I'm sure. Nobody's perfect. I noticed your mum likes to dabble in a little bit of the old racism, Chief Inspector.'

Bob bristled but let Carol continue talking.

'Am I a killer? Not since Gary Lineker was a footballer. I hear he does podcasts now, but doesn't everyone?'

'Why didn't you think to mention your past when we spoke the other day?' asked Laura.

'You didn't seem interested in much of anything I had to say. Besides, it's not my typical way of introducing myself. "Hello, my name is Carol. I'm a convicted serial killer." Here's a thought: if I did murder Desmond, why would I be insisting to you that it *was* a murder while you seemed to be under the impression that it wasn't? What would be the logic in that?'

'You killed seven people. You've admitted that,' said Laura, 'which doesn't seem particularly logical to me. Maybe you're the type to do illogical things.'

'I can assure you that each of those killings was perfectly logical.'

Carol looked at the cold brick wall, painted grey. Really, it could have been 1988 again. Her last interrogation had been south of the river but this might as well be the same room.

Back then there'd been an ashtray in the middle of the table, packed with stubs. No, lots had changed since then. No point pretending otherwise.

This time she was being interrogated by a woman, which made a nice change. The male detective, Bob Beattie, he didn't look healthy. Bags under his eyes, stubble on each of his chins. His hands were dry. Carol could see blood on his knuckles from where the skin had cracked. What was it that men of his age and type had against hand cream? He looked like he belonged in the days of her first police interview.

'What about Desmond? Was killing him logical?' asked Laura.

'For whoever did it, perhaps. But it wasn't me. If I were you, I'd think about the person for whom killing Desmond might have been logical.'

'*Whom.* You're smart, aren't you, Carol?' said Bob.

Carol didn't respond. What was she to say to that? A lady says 'whom' and now she's an evil genius?

'You take a baking class, is that right?' Laura asked.

Carol smiled. 'It's more of a club, really, but yes.'

'And does Desmond go to that same club?'

'Before he was pushed from a four-storey building, yes. He tended to leave early.'

'He left early?' said Laura.

'Yes. He usually did.'

'And why was that?' said Laura.

'You'd have to ask Desmond.'

'Desmond's dead,' said Laura.

'He said he was tired and left.'

'Did he try any of the cakes? The day before,' asked Laura.

'They weren't ready yet.' Carol looked down at Laura's notes.

'Is that it? The only evidence you have? That I'm a former killer who likes to bake? You must have some other unsolved murders. Why don't you chalk me down for them too?'

'You weren't seen with any of those victims the day before,' said Laura. 'You weren't the first to report their death.'

'This really is it,' said Carol. 'These are your only grounds.'

Laura exhaled through her nose. She appeared to be tiring of the jocular tone. 'I've been looking at your work history, Carol. You worked in a lab once, is that right?'

For the first time Carol felt a little unrooted. Where was this going? 'For a bit. On reception. About forty years ago. What of it?'

'You're familiar with poison, aren't you, Carol? One of your methods.'

'This is all a very long time ago.'

'Not everything is.'

Carol felt the mood shift. Did Laura think she was gaining the upper hand? Carol did her best to keep a poker face.

Laura rested her elbows on the table. 'You're not an entirely reformed woman, are you, Carol? When we arrested you last night you had a bottle at the throat of a woman.'

'You're right. That was terrible of me. I must apologise to Belinda when I next see her. Here's something that might be of use. Somebody told Belinda that I called her a slut. I did nothing of the sort. Somebody was trying to trigger me into violence.'

'Are you easily triggered into violence, Carol?'

Carol directed her eyes at the paint peeling off the ceiling and pondered the question seriously.

'No. I don't think I am, not any more. I don't know what got into me. It won't happen again.'

The door to the room opened and a young officer popped his head in. He looked at Bob. 'Excuse me, sorry. A quick word?'

Laura stood up quickly. 'I'll handle this.'

Laura exited, and Bob and Carol sat for moment.

'I didn't do it, Detective,' said Carol.

'We should wait until DS Welsh comes back.'

'If I did, I'd tell you.'

'Really, we should wait.'

'Sorry.'

They paused again but Carol couldn't help herself. 'Shep Newsom. Now, there's a man with a motive, who happened to be in the building at the time of the murder. I'm sure you already knew that.'

'Honestly, you're going to get me into trouble if you keep talking while she's not here.'

Carol nodded, clocking the office politics at play. 'Do you want me to stop?'

Bob narrowed his eyes, wrestling with the dilemma. 'No. Go on.'

'I'm sure you're also looking at Jim, you know, the former gangster? A man who knows how to kill, who was in the building, and who there's every reason to suspect had a gripe against a former Metropolitan Police chief. He even had a big row with Desmond a couple of nights before the murder. Let me think . . . Why else do people kill? For love? That's one, isn't it?

Well, Belinda claims to have been in love with Desmond, but just a few days later she's sprawled all over her new boyfriend. You're the experts but I'd say that's an avenue worth pursuing. The roof: that's locked. I'm sure you've taken a look, but you must be wondering why there's a lock to that door and who has the access.'

Bob shuffled uncomfortably.

'That points to Sheldon Oaks staff members, surely? I don't want to tell you how to do your jobs,' said Carol, 'but if I'm your number-one suspect, I'd say you may not be looking hard enough at the others.'

Bob got twitchy and started rolling a cigarette. 'This is weird. Being lectured on how to do my job by Carol Quinn. You're right, obviously. We've got no evidence. I just thought it had to be you, what with your track record and you being nearby. Maybe this is revealing too much, but you're smart so why not? I thought you'd have confessed by now.'

'Sorry, Bob, I only confess to things I did.'

'We do have one thing in our favour, though.'

'What's that?' said Carol, genuinely curious.

'People don't like serial killers. Politicians, traffic wardens, serial killers. They're the big three, right? Do you think anyone's gonna mind if we pin it on you? CPS don't want to be the ones to leave a serial killer in an old people's home. I don't think we're gonna have a problem getting a charge. Do you? So if I was you, Carol, I'd tone down the cockiness, I'd think twice before you slag off people's mums, and I'd start thinking about how embarrassing it's gonna be in a few years when you're the only lag walking around Bronzefield with a zimmer frame.'

Laura opened the door and beckoned Bob with her finger. He left the room.

Carol hardened, contemplating her tricky situation. She had no control over her own destiny. None.

There was a small pile of files on the desk in front of her. Looking at the door, she took one and opened it. The autopsy results, pictures from the scene. It was Desmond's murder file. Her pulse racing, Carol took her phone from her pocket and started taking pictures of each page.

She heard footsteps closing in on the door but managed to finish the job and stuff her phone back into her pocket just in time. She sat still and set her face into the most nonchalant expression she could muster.

Bob and Laura came back into the room with, to Carol's surprise, a familiar face. Margaret.

TWENTY-FOUR

Carol and Margaret walked out of the police station and headed into Hampstead village. Carol's eyes took a moment to adjust to the sun. Before they got to the high street, they made their way down a road with big, three-floor houses. Well-kept gardens, wide front doors, loft extensions. Each place must be worth millions, thought Carol. There was street after street after street of them. Where did all these people get their money? Carol told herself to be grateful for what she had.

'Thank you, Margaret. That was very kind of you.'

Margaret spoke fast. 'I can't believe I did it, really. I was sitting there this morning at breakfast. I don't know where Geoffrey and Catherine are. They didn't show up, probably sleeping in after last night. It all got a little much. Some of the men were drinking brandy and talking politics like it was the nineteenth century or something. But I was thinking to myself – I have to know what's going on. I suppose you think I'm an awful busybody. But I thought, Now hang on, I'm a QC, well, KC now, I suppose. I'm a bloody barrister. I was home secretary, for Heaven's sake – not that you'd think it, the way the men in the home go on and on about politics without thinking to ask me if they actually have a clue what they're talking about – but I thought, this is this morning that I thought ... perhaps Carol needs representation.'

'I really do appreciate it.'

'I'm glad I did because they can't just hold you like that. They've got no evidence! Or, if they have, they're not willing to show it.'

'Well, they might have *some*.'

Margaret touched Carol's shoulder. 'Oh, Jesus. You did it, didn't you, Carol?'

Carol laughed. There was something so charming about Margaret's ditsy energy. Hard to believe that this woman had once been ultimately responsible for the prison service that had confined her for so long. 'I didn't. But while I was in there I managed to have a look at the ... I suppose you'd call it a crime file? I took some pictures. Why don't we go back to my place and we can go through it all together?'

Margaret stopped. 'Oh dear.'

'What?'

'Carol, do you mind if I'm completely honest with you for a moment?'

'Please.'

'I'm a little scared to be alone with you, in your flat. Now, Catherine and Geoffrey, they seem convinced you did it. Geoffrey keeps talking about "hunches" and "no coincidences", and Catherine says you may be our friend but we have to look at the situation objectively. I don't know what I think. I've always been agnostic about everything anyway. Never settle on a view.

In politics, they used to call me wily but I think I've just always struggled to make up my mind.'

'I bet you were good at making speeches.'

'Was that a dig? It feels like a dig. I know I can talk too much. Am I talking too much?'

'No. Carry on, but maybe slow down a little.'

'Carol, I don't know if you did it,' said Margaret, deliberately. 'But I do believe in innocent until proven guilty.'

'Pleased to hear it.'

'What time is it?' asked Margaret.

Carol looked at her watch. 'Just after eleven.'

'Do you think the pubs are open yet?'

While Margaret bought their drinks, Carol sat at a table in the Flask and thought about how Hampstead provided an altogether different class of alcoholic. While the morning drinkers in the pubs of her South London youth read the *Racing Post* and the *Mirror*, here they read the *Telegraph*. On Walworth Road it was pints of lager or a double shot of Bell's. In Hampstead village it was a strong cask ale or a large glass of Merlot. The wealth around here afforded one the scenic route to cirrhosis of the liver.

This was the first pub Carol had been into since leaving prison. An awful lot had changed. No smoking for a start, which didn't feel right. Of the five senses, smell had always felt like the one you'd least like to have in a pub. The television in the corner played twenty-four-hour news. There were big round dark wood tables. No carpet, no fruit machines, no jukebox. On their table was bottle of balsamic vinegar. How odd. She looked at the menu in front of her.

BROAD BEAN, PEA AND DILL FRITTERS
WITH WHIPPED FETA. £14
SKATE, CRAB BISQUE, CORNISH EARLIES
AND SAMPHIRE. £22
HEREFORD ONGLET WITH BURNT SALSA ROJA
AND SOURED CREAM. £56 (FOR TWO TO SHARE)

Yes, a lot had changed.

'They put about five cubes of ice in yours. Is that okay?'

Margaret placed her gin and tonic and Carol's Bacardi and Coke on the table.

'Of course, thank you.'

'I hope you don't mind, I got us both doubles. I felt I needed it.'

'Perfect.' Carol took a sip. 'Right. Shall we take a look?'

'Oooh, yes.' Margaret shuffled next to her.

'Are you sure you're okay sitting next to me, Margaret? It's very quiet in here. I could stab you in the gut and make an easy escape.'

'Oh, don't be silly! There's plenty of fat before you'll get to any of my organs.'

They both giggled and Carol took out her phone. This gave Margaret pause. 'Are we sure we want to ... I mean, you obtained that file ... Isn't this illegal?'

Teasing, Carol let her finger hover over the photo on her phone. 'No, you're right, actually. Let's not look. I'll just delete it.'

'No, Carol, don't!'

Carol smiled and Margaret slapped her leg. It was clear that neither of them could resist digging in.

They soon discovered that it was difficult for the pair of them to see the photos of the files on Carol's phone at the same time, so she worked out how to send them to Margaret's tablet and they were able to look on there. They were rather proud of themselves for successfully completing that operation.

Much of the information they already knew. Margaret filled Carol in on everything they'd learnt from the autopsy. She said that, if Carol hadn't done it, it would be helpful for them both to have the full picture, and that if she had done it then, well, she knew it all already.

From the files, they picked up some interesting evidence about a thread of fibre found on Desmond's shirt. 'Wool. Not from the victim's own clothes' was scrawled next to a magnified picture. The thread was a fluorescent yellow.

One thing that struck them both as strange was that there were no photos of the roof. It was, after all, where the murder had taken place. Why were there no pictures?

They had to find a way of getting onto that roof. The answer to who had killed Desmond was surely there.

'If we do manage to get up there, do you promise not to push me off?' Margaret had a cheeky glint in her eye but Carol could sense some honesty in her request. She really was afraid of her. And fair enough. Less than twenty-four hours beforehand Carol had decided to take up killing again. But now she knew why. She'd felt alone. Sat here next to a woman of her own age, a woman she liked, Carol knew that all she needed to stop her from giving in to her most shameful vice was good friends.

'Margaret?' Carol fixed her eyes on her. She wanted to underline the importance of what she had to say.

'Yes?'

'I won't insult you by telling you I didn't kill Desmond again. That's something I have to prove to you. But, Margaret, I need your help in proving it. I can't do this on my own. You're all investigators – the whole home is filled with them. It's not a fair fight. I cannot go back to prison. This life . . .' Carol gestured at their surroundings, their morning drinking, in one of London's nicest neighbourhoods. 'I'm not sure you realise how lucky we are.'

'So, you want to take a look on the roof?' said Margaret.

TWENTY-FIVE

Geoffrey opened the door to Desmond's flat. No furniture, no pictures on the walls: the place was bare.

'We're too late.' Geoffrey's voice echoed in the space.

'I guess his daughter took all his things.' Catherine walked through the flat, stepping from one room to another. She entered a bedroom. 'There's a few boxes left in here. Do you think it would be bad of us to take a look?'

'Anything is justified if it gets you closer to the killer, Catherine.' Geoffrey found his old self returning. He was a detective again and it felt good. He noticed a red spot on the hardwood floor. Savouring the moment, he squatted, dabbed it with a finger. It was 1986 again and he was at the top of his game. He was a respected copper on the Met, had an active sex life, and went to the toilet no more than three or four times a day.

The spot was dry but Geoffrey remembered the colour well. It was dried blood.

'It's cakes,' said Catherine, from the other room. 'Boxes and boxes of cakes. I didn't know Desmond did so much baking!'

'Catherine, I may have found something of interest.'

With a jolt, Geoffrey was reminded that it wasn't 1986. Squatting had been a bad idea. The pain shot through him. 'Ow! Ow! Bloody ow! Jesus Christ! Bloody ow! My bloody knees! I think I'm stuck! My bloody knees!'

'I think I have something that might help with the pain,' said Catherine. 'These are cannabis cakes.'

Catherine sat on the floor next to Geoffrey and they agreed to share one small piece of cake. One small piece between the two of them shouldn't do much harm. Geoffrey suggested it might even help them to look at the case from a new perspective.

'Aren't you concerned? I mean, you were a police officer. It's illegal.'

'Catherine, I spent a year undercover. I'm afraid to say I've had my fair share of hashish. I built up a considerable level of tolerance. It's you I'm worried about.'

'Well, since we're being honest with each other, Geoffrey, I smoked rather a lot at a yoga retreat a couple of years ago,' she whispered in his ear. 'I used to do it all the time in the seventies.'

They each took a bite. Geoffrey commented that it was a little too dry. While they waited for the effects to roll in, they contemplated why the cakes were there. Who knew what went on behind people's front doors? Had Desmond been running a little operation? He'd never seemed to have much interest in the actual baking the group did but maybe he'd been doing some on the side. Rather a lot, in fact. Geoffrey had heard rumours about Desmond's corruption in the past, but it was hard to believe that he had been dealing drugs. If Desmond's daughter had cleared out the place and left the boxes, surely that meant she was in on it. Catherine had heard she was a piece of work. Her husband had owned a lot of businesses. Perhaps he had some kind of felonious bakery on the go and Desmond was the supplier. But for them to be a criminal family, running a drugs business out of an old people's home, it just seemed too wild to comprehend.

The room turned sepia and Catherine's body started to hum. Was the marijuana taking effect? Strong stuff. She felt that old paranoia. Geoffrey was talking about something but she couldn't focus.

'So, you see, this was the living room but now it's no longer a living room, Catherine, because no one is living in it, you know? It's just a room and what is a room but a box. Why are we naming rooms? I mean *bedroom*. It's only a bedroom once you put a bed in it, but the bed takes up space, you know, the more bed . . .' Geoffrey paused, apparently stunned by his own profundity '. . . the less *room*.'

'I suddenly feel very stoned,' said Catherine.

'Oh, really?' said Geoffrey. 'I don't think it's affecting me.'

'You said you'd found something interesting,' said Catherine.

'Huh?'

'Before you hurt your knee, you said you'd found something interesting.'

'Over there,' said Geoffrey. 'Look at the floor. There's a speck of blood. We should probably collect a sample.'

Catherine walked over to the spot Geoffrey was pointing at. She took tweezers from her handbag and scraped up a speck. She inspected it closely, then sniffed. A fit of giggles hit her.

'What?'

'This is . . .' she struggled to get out the words '. . . this is ketchup.'

Now they were both in hysterics, laughing like they hadn't done in decades, laughing at the absurdity of the situation. Two retirees, stupidly high, in the middle of what was supposed to be a covert murder investigation. Catherine sat down against the wall, beside Geoffrey. They looked at each other, sharing the moment. Catherine felt she could see Geoffrey, truly see him, the man behind all the nonsense, all the desperation to prove how clever he was. She could see that it came from an endearing vulnerability. He was a sweet man.

He kissed her on the lips. 'Sorry, Catherine. I just think you're quite lovely.'

She smiled. 'No, it's fine.'

They were silent again, their eyes still connected.

'How are your knees feeling?' said Catherine.

Geoffrey stood up. 'I think they're all right. Wonder drug. Did you say you had a key to Carol's flat?'

'Yes.'

'We should take a look now.'

Walking down the corridor, Geoffrey and Catherine held on to each other for support. Going out into the world was frightening. They didn't want to be seen, not in this state.

Elisa walked by, heading in the direction they'd come from.

'Hello!' she said cheerfully. They looked at the floor and mumbled back. Catherine held onto her handbag, tightly.

They were on their way to investigate Carol's flat when Geoffrey mentioned that he had the munchies and their priorities changed. Holding on to each other, trying their very best to look sober and normal, the pair took the lift downstairs and headed for the Apple Tree.

With lunchtime nearly over there was hardly anyone in the restaurant but to Catherine and Geoffrey it looked like a terrifying mass of people. The truth was that they were too stoned to do something as taxing as sitting down at a table and ordering something to eat. They stood at the edge of the restaurant, staring at it as if it were an obstacle course beyond their current capabilities.

'I've an idea,' Geoffrey whispered.

He crept along the wall in the direction of the kitchen's swinging double doors. Catherine followed, tiptoeing like a child at a sleepover on a midnight snack run.

'I'm sure there's some bread we can grab in here,' he said. 'We'll leave an IOU.'

It was only when they found themselves in the kitchen that the absurdity of what they were doing dawned on Catherine. They had apartments full of food, there was even a communal kitchen. Why were they conducting an SAS raid on the restaurant? Whatever tolerance she had once had for class B drugs had entirely faded away.

To Catherine's relief, there was nobody in the kitchen. She scanned the counters for a loaf of bread or, in the absolute best-case scenario, a bowl of chips. Her highly disciplined diet was on pause.

'Will this do?'

Geoffrey was holding a raw potato. Even in her state, she was able to recognise that they could surely do better.

But then something caught Catherine's eye. A folder on the counter labelled 'Weekly Meal Plan'. From out of nowhere, she found focus, a moment of clarity. They were supposed to be investigating a murder but had, all of a sudden, turned themselves into wild-eyed potheads, trawling the building for food. In that folder there might be a clue as to how Desmond had been killed.

She fumbled through it, looking for Saturday. There it was. Shepherd's pie. On the day that Desmond died, the Apple Tree had been serving shepherd's pie, his last meal, according to the autopsy. Why had they been fixated on that lick of Carol's spoon? Surely this was the more obvious explanation. No slow-release poisons, or somehow contaminating the spoon but not the cake mixture itself. That didn't add up, did it? Why had they so quickly accepted that Carol was the murderer? Innocent until proven guilty, and as far as they knew she was nowhere near being charged. She could be on her way back to Sheldon Oaks right now, for all they knew.

Someone working in the restaurant could easily have poisoned Desmond's meal. Once that had failed, they could have strangled him, hit him, pushed him off the roof. If they were staff they would certainly know how to get up there. But who?

Just then, there was a loud clatter of pans falling to the floor, making Catherine and Geoffrey jump in terror. Of course the kitchen wasn't empty. How could they have been so stupid? They looked up to see not a chef but Belinda walking around the corner of the L-shaped space, with dishevelled hair. She saw them and adjusted her skirt, a post-coital glow written all over her face. Following sheepishly behind her was Marco, the waiter.

No one knew quite what to say. Each couple had been caught by the other in the act of doing something wrong.

Geoffrey broke the silence. 'I'll pay you ten pounds for this potato.'

TWENTY-SIX

After the drama of downstairs, Catherine and Geoffrey decided to proceed with Plan A and made their way to Carol's empty flat. As Catherine turned the key in the door something told her they were being incredibly stupid. Carol could have been released by the police for all they knew. Catherine's brain was foggy. She'd forgotten how much stronger a hash cake could be than a couple of puffs on a joint. They'd had a whole slice each!

They made their way inside. No noise but the tick of a clock on the wall.

Catherine told Geoffrey her thoughts on the shepherd's pie: Carol might not be the murderer after all. She could see in Geoffrey's face that he was suffering the effects too and not really capable of taking in what she had to say.

Catherine clapped her hands together. 'Okay, where shall we start?'

'Hard to say,' said Geoffrey, trying to activate his brain. 'Hard to say. I'm going to sit down for a second.' He fell back onto Carol's sofa. Catherine was not in the mood to sit down. When she'd smoked dope regularly, back in the seventies, she'd often got a lot done while stoned. She was just one of those people. There were those who passed out and there were those who moved about. She was the latter.

Geoffrey closed his eyes and Catherine started to potter around Carol's flat. There wasn't much to look at. Carol didn't appear to be one for clutter. Everybody else's place here had piles and piles of stuff they couldn't get rid of. Carol, Catherine supposed, hadn't really had the chance to accumulate junk.

When you bought a place at Sheldon Oaks, you had the option to buy it furnished, which Carol had apparently done. Catherine felt sorry for her. The flat was sanitary; it lacked character. Generic framed prints of middle-of-the-road paintings on the walls, uniform crockery, six mugs, all the same. It told the story of a life not led.

Catherine pushed open the door to Carol's bedroom, reminding herself of the noble reason why she was there: she wasn't being intrusive, she was getting to the bottom of a murder. If Carol hadn't done it, then Catherine might be about to clear her name. On Carol's bedside table there were some books. Catherine sat on the edge of the bed and picked them up. Some puzzle books and a pen. A couple of well-thumbed crime thrillers set in Exeter.

Catherine felt something against her heel, under the bed. She bent over, scared by what she might find. A body? It was a cardboard box. Full of limbs? She could hear Geoffrey snoring from the other room. Catherine slid the box out between her legs and opened it.

The box was full of black hardback A4 journals. Catherine

took one from the top and turned to the first page. It was hard to catch her breath.

'Geoffrey! Geoffrey, come in here! You need to see this!'

Her mouth moved but no voice would come out.

TWENTY-SEVEN

kill. kill. kill. kill. kill. kill. kill. kill. kill. kill. kill.
kill. kill. kill. kill. kill. kill. kill. kill. kill. kill. kill.
kill. kill. kill. kill. kill. kill. kill. kill. kill. kill. kill.
kill. kill. kill. kill. kill. kill. kill. kill. kill. kill. kill.
kill. kill. kill. kill. kill. kill. kill. kill. kill. kill. kill.
kill. kill. kill. kill. kill. kill. kill. kill. kill. kill. kill.
kill. kill. kill. kill. kill. kill. kill. kill. kill. kill. kill.
kill. kill. kill. kill. kill. kill. kill. kill. kill. kill. kill.
kill. kill. kill. kill. kill. kill. kill. kill. kill. kill. kill.
kill. kill. kill. kill. kill. kill. kill. kill. kill. kill. kill.
kill. kill. kill. kill. kill. kill. kill. kill. kill. kill. kill.
kill. kill. kill. kill. kill. kill. kill. kill. kill. kill. kill.
kill. kill. kill. kill. kill. kill. kill. kill. kill. kill. kill.
kill. kill. kill. kill. kill. kill. kill. kill. kill. kill. kill.
kill. kill. kill. kill. kill. kill. kill. kill. kill. kill. kill.
kill. kill. kill. kill. kill. kill. kill. kill. kill. kill. kill.
kill. kill. kill. kill. kill. kill. kill. kill. kill. kill. kill.
kill. kill. kill. kill. kill. kill. kill. kill. kill. kill. kill.
kill. kill. kill. kill. kill. kill. kill. kill. kill. kill. kill.

kill. kill.

That was the first page. A disturbing read sober, a suffocating nightmare on your first hash cake in fifty years.

At least the journals contained some variety: drawings of mutilated bodies, dark poetry, long, detailed, violent fantasies. Or were they testimonies? Was Carol simply documenting what she had done?

There were scrapbooks filled with newspaper reports of murders. Surely Carol hadn't done them all. Some of the dates and places didn't match up. As sick a mind as Carol had, it would be hard to pin the assassination of JFK on her.

Carol was a fanatic and this was her life's work, her love letter to murder.

There were practical diagrams offering advice on the most effective parts of the body to stab. There were lists of poisons, with the required dosages noted beside them. Catherine had to admire the work. Carol had done her research.

There was a long list of murder methods, each with a paragraph on the pros and cons – drowning, shooting, stabbing, strangling, poisoning, pushing, bludgeoning, impaling, drilling.

The work was thorough. Hand drills were harder to clean than axes; axes created more splatter and required a good aim. Poisoning was like baking, a science, not an art form. Drowning and pushing, when done right, left no murder weapon but 'may require muscle'. Strangling offered one the opportunity to look into the victim's eyes, the chance to watch them die up close. This could be a pro or a con, depending on the circumstances.

Catherine felt like insects were crawling around her body. She was in the bedroom of a serial killer, sifting through their thoughts. She wanted to wake Geoffrey but she couldn't move.

One page described a man in a warehouse, tied up, lying on a concrete floor. Carol placed a hot iron on his chest, his screams fading into the distance as she went to run some errands. She returned just before the iron touched the concrete, proud with herself for timing it just right. Catherine was cold, chilled to think that she shared a world with a mind like this.

And then a key turned in the door.

TWENTY-EIGHT

Carol and Margaret's stroll back to Sheldon Oaks was leisurely, their drinks providing them each with a pleasant buzz. Once they entered the grounds, rather than taking the most direct route to the building's entrance they took a detour around the gardens, agreeing that they didn't appreciate their beautiful surroundings enough.

Dozens of bees were working away. It gave Carol pleasure to see nature in action, oblivious to the city beyond the gates. She caught a whiff of a familiar scent.

'What's that smell?' said Margaret.

Carol pointed to its source.

'Ah. I see,' said Margaret, spotting Tyler, who was hiding under a tree, smoking a spliff. 'Back when I was in charge that could get you a custodial sentence. Silly, really.'

The lawns were yellowing in the patches that the sprinklers couldn't reach. When was the last time it had rained? Carol ran her hand along some pampas grass. She picked a small piece and crumbled it in her fingers. She remembered the feeling from when she'd first done it, seventy years ago.

Margaret talked Carol through the species on display: pink dahlias, foxgloves, deadly nightshade hiding among the salvias and the lupines, the monkshood and the asters.

'How do you know all this?' asked Carol.

'Boarding school. Never had too many companions, I'm afraid,' said Margaret. 'Gardens were lovely, though. Made friends with the flowers.'

Carol looked at her and wondered if they would have got on as children. They'd grown up in very different worlds but were both eccentrics who didn't quite fit in. Yes, she thought. They probably would have done.

Both women jumped with fright. A faceless figure slowly emerged from a row of hedges, a white silhouette, gaining in size as it walked in their direction.

'Hello, ladies.'

Only then did they identify the figure as a beekeeper. They laughed and headed for the main entrance.

'I'm pretty sure they have a skeleton key here that has access to all our apartments,' said Carol.

'It would make sense, I suppose,' said Margaret.

'Could well work for the lock on the door to the roof too.'

'Could do, yes,' said Margaret. 'But how do we get hold of one without arousing suspicion?'

'Here's a plan. We go back to my apartment. I can keep my front door open if that puts you at ease,' said Carol. Margaret playfully slapped her arm. 'Then I call down to Reception. Better yet, I press my alarm. That should send Elisa, and who-ever else is about, upstairs. Meanwhile, you make your way to what should be an empty front desk for a snoop around. I'm sure there's a key in a drawer down there. I doubt it'll be hard to find.'

'I don't know,' said Margaret, playing nervously with the zip on her handbag.

'If you don't find it, you don't find it. I'll just say I felt faint, they'll give me a glass of water and we'll come up with another plan.'

'I don't know about snooping around. I'm not . . . Carol, that's not really my scene.'

'You were a politician, yes?'

'Yes.'

'A successful one. In cabinet?'

'Yes.'

'Well, doesn't that involve a little lying, a little bending the truth, a little bit of the dark arts?'

'I always tried to keep myself human but, well, yes.' Margaret looked around to see if anyone was listening, then leant in and whispered, 'I've got top secret clearance. I used to read people's MI5 files. They know *everything*. You wouldn't believe some of the things people get up to. I couldn't look the foreign secretary in the face after I found out what he liked to get up to at the weekend.'

Carol raised her eyebrows.

'Leather. Lots of leather,' said Margaret. 'But that's all I'll say. My lips are sealed.'

'Then think of this like that. A little bit of the dark arts for the greater good.'

Margaret sighed, conceding Carol's argument. 'All right. If it's for the greater good.'

They passed Elisa, who was alone at Reception going through some paperwork. Carol and Margaret moved through the lobby quickly, keeping their heads down. Polly was in an armchair near the lifts, with a pot of tea and a bag of yarn.

'That woman is always knitting,' mumbled Margaret.

'Cup of coffee, before we put our plan into motion? Perhaps something stronger for courage?' said Carol.

'Why not?'

They travelled up to Carol's floor in the lift. Margaret said she could feel her morning G and T in her legs. Carol turned the key in her front door.

TWENTY-NINE

Giles Temple shut the door to his office and climbed out of his beekeeping suit. His back was sticky with sweat. Installing a shower in here was a nice idea but how much would that cost? He needed incomings, not outgoings. Black, not red. Giles Temple needed a miracle.

How did other people do it? How did they keep their heads above water? Was it a case of the swan's legs? Were they hiding their frantic paddling?

It wasn't as if Giles hadn't been dealt a good hand. He'd boarded at Eton. Oxbridge had been a stretch, but he'd managed to get himself into St Andrews and a ruddy good time he'd had there too, as president of the Drinking and Shagging Society. Then a couple of years of travelling – eight to be exact.

When he'd finally arrived back in Blighty, he'd found his dad waiting for him, unimpressed by the depth of his son's tan, hands on hips. 'What are you going to *do*, Giles?' His friends were all making good progress in finance, well on their way to an early retirement, and his working life hadn't even got started. A couple of years (twelve to be exact) running a restaurant in

Fulham followed. His dad had put up the money, told him not to fuck it up, and when his dad had finally cut him off, when the bailiffs had finally caught up with Giles, his father's hands had rested on his hips again. 'You're on your own now, old boy.'

And then something wonderful happened: Giles's father died.

His sister got the country house, but Giles got Sheldon Oaks. He'd never have to worry about money again. To tell the truth, he'd never worried about money before. That, in fact, had been the problem all along. It was now, only now, that his money worries would start.

The place had run successfully as a high-class home for the elderly for thirty years. 'Don't tinker with it and you can't go wrong,' his dad's accountant had told him. But Giles had had ideas. His dad had been too conservative, too stuck in the past. Giles would be an innovator, bring luxury living for the aged into the twenty-first century. Perhaps, if he was ambitious enough, if he had a good tail wind, he could even get it into the twenty-second. In the first year, he splashed around cash like it had no value. A sauna, a pool, state-of-the-art DJ decks, a climbing wall. 'This is an old people's home,' his sister had reminded him, but Giles knew best. He'd travelled, he'd seen the world, he knew a thing or two. He was *investing*. Elderly people don't know they want a state-of-the-art sprung-floor martial-arts studio until you give them one. He borrowed money against the value of the property and skipped all the meetings with his accountant. And now it was all coming back to bite.

There's an inexhaustible supply of old people, he'd thought. The conveyor-belt runs in one direction: they'll keep coming.

And they did, but not enough. The numbers didn't add up any more and he was in deep trouble, looking desperately for a way out. Selling up wouldn't even pay off the debts, let alone leave him – a man without a CV worth wiping your arse with – any cash of his own.

Sometimes he'd slope off to a Wetherspoons during the day and look at the patrons. Could he just become one of them? They seemed happy enough. But when Giles stared at his bedroom ceiling at four in the morning, he couldn't even work out how to fund *that* lifestyle. How do they do it? How do they live? How does *anyone* do it?

Supplementary income. 'Side hustles' was what they called it. That would get him out of his mess. The latest idea was honey, but after spending thousands on the suit, the equipment, the hive, he was coming to realise that he had no idea how to grow or sell it. He knew you could get about ten pounds a pot from gullible tourists in Borough Market. Not bad. If he could just find a route to zero overheads and zero tax, then all he needed to sell to get back in the black was one million pots of honey.

Giles Temple butted his head against the wall. And then again. And then again.

THIRTY

'Geoffrey?' Carol said his name in a way that asked all the questions at once. What are you doing in my flat? Why are you asleep on my sofa? Who the fuck do you think you are?

Geoffrey opened his eyes, clearly not entirely sure where he was. The wide-awake Catherine walked out from the bedroom with a lamp in her hand. She waved it in the direction of Carol, like she was fending off a crocodile. 'Geoffrey, we need to get out of here right now.'

'Oh, let's not be silly, shall we?' said Margaret. 'There's safety in numbers. What are you both doing in Carol's flat?'

'Margaret, you don't understand,' said Catherine, her voice trembling. 'This woman is a *monster*.'

'Catherine, that's unkind,' said Margaret. 'What happened to Christian forgiveness? I thought better of you.'

'What were you doing in my room, Catherine?' said Carol, quietly.

'I've seen your box.'

'As the actress said to the—'

'Geoffrey, shut up,' snapped Catherine. 'Carol, you – you need to be locked up.'

Carol felt exposed. How dare she? 'Those are my private things.'

'I can see why you'd want to keep them private,' said Catherine.

Margaret had a question: 'What's in the box?'

'Brad Pitt. From that film, what was it? *Se7en. What's in the booooox?*'

'GEOFFREY! SHUT UP!' all three ladies shouted in unison.

'Sorry, I'm a little stoned, would you believe?'

'Margaret, you won't like this, but I've been reading Carol's diaries,' said Catherine.

'You're right. I don't. I'm not sure there's anything more sacrosanct than the privacy of a woman's diary.'

Carol was sure she'd seen Margaret's diaries for sale in a Waterstones before.

Catherine threw a journal at Margaret. It landed at her feet.

'I'm not reading it.'

'*Read it.*'

Carol found herself admiring Catherine's power. The yoga and granola lady had some spunk. She was planted, broad-shouldered, ready to fight.

Margaret picked up the journal and opened it, unable to disobey Catherine's instruction.

The room awaited Margaret's response. She retched. Well, that's unflattering, thought Carol.

'What bit are you reading?' asked Carol.

'You're biting off a man's nose.'

'There's a context to that.'

'Oh, yes? What's the context?' asked Catherine.

'He was a total shit.'

'Carol, this is horrifying,' said Margaret, unable to stop reading.

'This is . . .' Carol found the injustice of it all upsetting '. . . this is, well, it's just unfair. This was a period of my life. It was a hobby. We're judging people for their hobbies now, are we? That's okay, is it? I'm sorry, I know we're all of a certain age, but you lot need to do some reading. This is— I believe it's what the youngsters call kink-shaming. Catherine, I don't judge you for your yoga, do I? Or your swimming? Besides, and I cannot stress this enough, *this was all in the past.* You all *knew* I'd been a killer. What were you expecting to find in my old journals?'

'I was thinking of you as more of a cosy-crime killer, if I'm honest,' said Catherine. 'I thought you were like someone out of a Richard Osman novel. Those diaries, they're more Stephen King.'

Margaret was still leafing through the diary. 'Carol, you ate someone's liver?'

'I. WAS. HUNGRY.'

'I can't believe the police let you go. It's not safe. You're a beast,' said Catherine. The lamp was by her side now but she still looked prepared to strike Carol with it, should she need to.

'Well, um, I might have had something to do with that,' said Margaret, sheepishly. 'I, well, I went down to the police station and told them to release her.'

'Margaret!' exclaimed Catherine.

'Well, I hadn't read this, had I?'

'Yes, but you knew she was a killer.'

Geoffrey, who was still on the sofa, held up his hand. 'I'm not being funny, Catherine, but you did say earlier on that you thought maybe she hadn't done it after all.'

'Can you not refer to me as "she", please? I'm right here. This is ... well, it's just bigotry, isn't it? You should be ashamed of yourselves. And you still haven't explained why you're in my flat. What gives you the right?'

'I wasn't sure about it,' said Catherine. 'You'd been arrested and I just wanted to know if you'd done it and, if you did do it, why. And now I have my answer: because you're deranged. You belong in an institution.'

The words hurt. Carol was not a psychopath. She was a woman with feelings.

'Come on, Geoffrey. Let's get out of here,' said Catherine.

Geoffrey, still apparently dazed, stood up. 'Carol, I'm suddenly a little peckish. You don't happen to have any biscuits, do you?'

'Geoffrey!' Catherine grabbed him by the wrist.

She and Geoffrey edged towards the front door, keeping their distance, their eyes on Carol. Margaret had already left the flat. Once they had a clear route to the exit, Catherine put down the lamp. Then she and Geoffrey ran as fast as two people of their age could.

The door shut behind her and Carol was alone again. The walls were closing in on her and they wouldn't stop until they formed a cell.

*

Carol sat down at her kitchen table and stared into space. Her palms rested on the table's cold surface. She felt vulnerable and exposed. It was embarrassing for people to see her innermost thoughts. Did other people really not go through a phase like that? Granted, maybe they didn't carry any of it out, but surely everyone had fantasised about beheading the annoying man on the bus.

She had no time to dwell. That was what the last few decades had been about. Carol Quinn had done enough staring into space for a hundred lifetimes. Now was the time to fight for the life she had. If people were afraid of her, *good*. She'd use that to her advantage. She'd interview her suspects. She'd get them alone and she'd interrogate them. Bad cop. If everyone thought she was liable to kill them at a moment's notice, that meant they'd do what she said. 'Sit down, let's talk.'

She heard a vacuum cleaner outside. Carol looked at her watch. Around the same time that Desmond had come off the roof. No time like the present. There was a cleaner and they needed to be questioned.

Then something came back to her.

The vacuuming stopped. Good. A gentle breeze, a touch of sun on her face.

Why had the sound of the Hoover stopped just before Desmond was killed?

THIRTY-ONE

Carol recognised Elisa from behind. She was bent over, vacuuming in a tight black skirt and flats with a black suit jacket. Some people vacuumed in neat lines, like they were mowing a lawn. Elisa attacked the floor in short jabs that went in all directions.

'Hello, Elisa,' said Carol. Elisa didn't hear her at first. Carol turned off the Hoover with her foot. Elisa jumped.

'Surprised to see me?'

'Carol! I thought you were . . .'

'In police custody? Just as you planned it?' Carol wasn't messing about. The Henry Hoover's face remained in a fixed smile, oblivious to the tension in the air.

'Carol, I didn't—'

'No, you didn't call the police – Geoffrey Standing did that – but you did tell Belinda I'd called her a slut. Didn't you? When you knew I hadn't? You knew that the police were on their way, I'm sure they called ahead, so you engineered an altercation between me and Belinda. Bet you were delighted when the police arrived just as it kicked off.'

'Carol, I—'

'You and I are going to talk, Elisa, and we're going to talk now. In private.'

Elisa nodded.

'In my flat?' suggested Carol.

'Giles's office would be better, if you don't mind. He's gone out for a while. It's just along here.'

Carol followed.

Elisa pushed open the door to the office and a stack of papers toppled over. The room set Carol on edge. She'd always kept a tidy cell; this place was chaos. At the back of the office there was a desk with an old Mac desktop computer and piles of detritus. An apple core, protein-bar wrappers, unopened letters with red ink. Behind the desk there was a door, presumably to a cupboard. On the floor a golf bag lay on its side beside a putting mat. Elisa moved a box off a chair. 'Sorry, sit down.'

'Thank you.'

Tyler popped his head around the door. 'Mum.'

'I'm sorry, Carol. Give me a moment.'

Elisa left the room and had a conversation with Tyler in the corridor. Carol nosily picked up a stack of papers and skimmed through it. When Elisa returned she put the papers down.

'That boy. He never stops thinking about karaoke night. Wants to be a DJ,' said Elisa, rolling her eyes. She sat at the other side of the desk and noted Carol taking in the state of the room. 'You see what I have to deal with?'

'Why were you vacuuming? I thought you had a cleaner.'

Elisa picked up a stack of bills and waved them. 'We can't afford her.'

'But I thought . . .'

'That this was a luxury retirement home? It's a disaster.'

'Why are you showing me this?' asked Carol.

'By way of an explanation. Carol, I'm sorry for what happened last night. I'm trying to show you the kind of pressure we're under here.' Elisa slowed down, emphasising her point. 'You *are* a problem, Carol. A very big problem. We were already struggling to find new residents. Why do you think we allowed a serial killer to buy an apartment? We were desperate. But then there's a murder. Did you do it, by the way?'

'No.'

'Carol. *Did you do it?*'

'Why does everybody keep asking me that? *No.*'

'It almost doesn't matter. The murder is already in the papers. When they find out we have you here, we'll never sell another apartment. I had to do something! I had to get you out of here. If you happened to be the murderer, great. That would be two problems solved.' Elisa spoke softly, conspiratorially. 'When I knew the police were on their way, I thought I'd give them a little bit more to work with. So, yes, I did tell Belinda you called her a slut. I'm sorry. Maybe it was wrong but . . .' She opened her arms to the state of the room. 'We're dealing with a lot.'

'You can't get rid of me. I have rights.'

There was a pause. The ladies looked at each other. There was an unsaid respect. Elisa was too impressive a woman to be in her current situation, thought Carol. Too elegant to have a boss who kept his office like this. But she'd seen a lot of women in prison who were too good for where they were, usually dragged down by the men in their lives.

'You just work here, yes?' asked Carol. 'I mean, you don't have a stake in Sheldon Oaks, do you?'

'No. I just work here, you're right.'

'Then why are you so concerned? You're a smart lady. You can get a job anywhere else, surely.'

'I love this place. It's beautiful, don't you think? I wish I could retire here.'

'Maybe you can.'

Elisa laughed. 'You think I can afford to retire here?'

'How long have you lived here? In London, I mean.'

'Twenty years. Or so.'

'Where did you come from? If you don't mind me asking. Is that question all right? I'm never sure.'

'Portugal.'

'Beautiful country. That's what I've heard, anyway.'

'You have to see it to believe it.'

Carol felt a pang of regret: her last passport had expired in the eighties. Sure, she could travel now. Maybe a cruise. That's what ladies of her age were supposed to do, but when she tried to picture it, it struck her as a prison on water. Would the entertainment be any better than the slam poets and ramshackle theatre companies who used to give their ever-so-earnest performances at Bronzefield?

Elisa held up her phone and showed Carol a picture. 'Ferragudo. My home town.' Her eyes shone with pride.

Carol took the phone for a closer look. An idyllic fishing village, boats, pretty houses with terracotta roofs, the green water twinkling in the bright sunlight. She felt suddenly aware that her time on Earth was finite. There was so much she'd never do now, so much she'd never see. 'Lovely,' she said. 'Why did you come here?'

'I don't know.' Elisa took back her phone and gazed at Ferragudo. 'I was young, looking for something, I guess.'

'Did you find it?'

'I got pregnant. It was very difficult for me. I had to work. Sometimes life just doesn't go the way you expect it to.'

It was a neat summary. Carol had learnt to do this over the years, to draw people's pasts out of them. Give them the opportunity and all people really wanted to talk about was themselves.

'I'll be fifty next year,' Elisa said mournfully.

Carol tried not to get annoyed at someone so much younger than her talking as if her life was drawing to a conclusion. She had to remind herself that this wasn't a podcast but an interrogation. 'Were you vacuuming last week, Elisa?'

'What? I don't know.'

'Just before Desmond was pushed off the roof, someone was vacuuming in the corridor. Was it you?'

Elisa blinked, running it through in her head. 'No. We let the cleaner go this week. That wouldn't have been me.'

'Where were you when the murder took place?'

'I would have been downstairs on the front desk, I'm sure.'

'And is there anyone who can verify that?'

'I'm sure there is. People saw me. You can ask around. So, you're investigating the murder now, are you, Carol?'

'Only way to clear my name is to find the killer.'

'Who are your suspects?'

Carol took a moment. Who *were* her suspects? She had a few, but perhaps now was the time to solidify them into some kind of list. 'I'd rather not say, if you don't mind.'

'Am I one?'

Carol smiled. 'Of course.'

'Why would I kill Desmond?'

'I was hoping you could tell me.'

Elisa rolled a pen back and forth on the desk. 'Have you thought about Polly?'

'*Polly?*'

'There's a lot more than meets the eye with that lady.'

'Oh? She writes novels, yes?'

'That's right. Crime novels. Knows a lot about murder.'

'Doesn't make her a murderer.'

'Write what you know. Isn't that what they say?'

Had that occurred to the police? wondered Carol. Should they be raiding book festivals? Taking DNA samples from the top crime writers and checking them against their unsolved murders? Carol had heard Richard Madeley was writing crime novels now. There was definitely *something* not quite right about that man.

'More than meets the eye, eh? I've met a few murderers, more than you I'd say, and she doesn't seem the type.'

'Neither do you,' said Elisa.

'Thank you.' Carol liked Elisa. She had a twinkle in her eye. Carol returned it with a twinkle of her own. 'Come on, then, why should I be looking at Polly? Other than the fact she writes about murder. It doesn't feel like a lot to go on.'

'Because of her past, I suppose. I shouldn't say . . . I'm not sure anybody else knows. It was a long time ago.'

Carol left a pause. An amateur might rush in with 'What past?' but that would give Elisa a question she could choose not to answer. Leaving silence was better. People don't like dead air. A good piece of gossip burnt a hole in the pocket. Carol stayed still until Elisa looked up and met her eyes.

'Polly used to be married to Desmond.'

THIRTY-TWO

Laura Welsh stood at the bar in the Unicorn. It was starting to fill up, the leisurely afternoon crowd swapping with the thirstier after-work drinkers. Punters were closing their laptops and ending the pretence that they were in the pub to do some work. That was the thing about North London: every public space was filled with people pretending to work. But working hours were over, even for those who were kidding themselves that they were writing a screenplay, and it was time to have some fun. A bar girl was fiddling with a remote control, trying to find the right sports channel for a demanding man in shorts and a polo shirt.

Like nearly all London pubs, the Unicorn had been infected with the gastro disease (the menu offered baked Camembert), but it still maintained some boozer charm. Intermittently, Laura heard the sound of pool balls clattering onto the table for another game.

She was pissed off to be buying the first round but that was the way it went. The youngest in Major Crimes always bought the first round. Never mind that the youngest was on the worst salary, never mind that the youngest wouldn't be staying long enough for the four other coppers to buy her a drink in return. In the Met, those were the rules and anyone not playing by them was a wrong 'un, not doing their time. When some of these blokes had been at the bottom of the ladder, you could still buy a round for a tenner. Now? In London? Five drinks cost the price of a flight to Sharm el-Sheikh, which is what she wished she was on.

Her friend Ruby had sent her a last-minute deal, suggested she join her for a week in an okay-looking three-star all-inclusive. The food would probably have been shit, endless buffets of suspiciously coloured pastries, but some sun would have been nice. Laura had said she couldn't get out of work. What she hadn't said was that it was her choice. She could have easily got the time off, she had some leave owed to her, but Laura wanted to solve this case. Something about it had got hold of her. Something about the way Bob had reacted when he'd seen that it was Sir Desmond Crisp who'd died. Laura had to know the whole truth and she feared that, if she left, maybe she never would.

There was something else too. The Carol Quinn interview had been a disaster. The old lady had pulled their pants down. They'd had no evidence and Carol had known it. Laura had thought they'd had the right woman; it had to be her. A serial killer arrives at a retirement home and someone gets murdered? Carol was going to confess and Laura Welsh was going to be the woman who drew it out of her. A high-profile case and Laura would be at the centre of it; word would spread around the Met that there was a hotshot new detective on the scene who had made the monster crumble. No one would stop Laura's rise.

But it hadn't worked out that way. Laura picked up her tray of pints and put three bags of crisps into her mouth.

'No smoky bacon?' said DI Pauline Crouch, in her gravel-voiced Geordie, as Laura arrived at the pub table.

'Sorry, I went for three plain.'

Pauline took a bag for herself, unimpressed. Pauline was a legend and a bitch. She wasn't interested in helping the women she'd blazed a trail for. Some people left a ladder, others took it away. Pauline trod on your fingers.

DI Trev Pickle waved a pack of fags. 'Ciggie?'

Pauline and DI Steve Talbott stood up.

Laura looked to Bob. 'You not going out?'

'Given up.'

'You've smoked five today.'

'Well, I'm giving up again.'

'I'm proud of you. It's your willpower that blows me away.'

'Nice patter,' said Pauline. 'You two shagging each other?'

'Fuck off, Pauline,' said Laura.

Pauline raised her eyebrows. *'Touché.'*

Once she and Bob were on their own, Laura took her chance and asked the question that had been on her mind. 'Why haven't we been on the roof?'

'Eh? They got a roof garden? Probably no seats but we can go when they get back if you like.'

'I don't mean here,' said Laura. 'I mean at Sheldon Oaks.'

Bob opened a bag of crisps and took a handful. 'Let's not talk about work.'

'Fine.' Laura took a big gulp of her Guinness. 'I guess I'll see you tomorrow.'

'No, no, no,' Bob pleaded, as Laura put her phone into her pocket, moving to leave. 'Why you got the hump?'

'Why haven't we been on the roof, Bob?'

He took a cigarette from his pocket and put it into his mouth. 'I have.'

'You have?'

'Yeah. On the first day. When you were finishing things with the body, I went up there.'

'Oh. Why's there no mention of it in the file?'

'Because there was nothing to report.'

'Nothing?'

'Honestly, babe. Nothing. No footprints. It was dry. No nothing. We swept the whole fucking thing. It's just a roof.'

'If you say so.'

Bob narrowed his eyes. 'What do you mean if I say so?'

'I mean if you say so. I trust you.' Laura shrugged. 'You know, some women might not like their work colleague calling them "babe".'

Bob scanned her, checking how serious she was. 'Yeah, but you're not like that, are you? It's just how I talk, innit?'

She shrugged again.

Uncomfortable, Bob changed the subject. 'You got a light?'

Laura shook her head. He got up and went for the door.

Laura took her phone back out of her pocket. Ruby had arrived at the hotel. She'd posted a picture of a cocktail by a pool, in front of a setting sun. The caption read, 'I guess this will just have to do for the week ;-).' I bet that drink's watered down, thought Laura, telling herself she'd made the right choice to stay in town.

She went to her email. Ten from companies she really should get around to unsubscribing from and then something interesting: a reply from a yarn shop in Falmouth, Cornwall.

Dear DS Welsh,

Thank you for your enquiry. Most of our business is in person but we do have a few online customers. You are correct that the particular yarn you asked about is only available at our store. We have one customer in London. Her name is Polly Slaughter. We deliver to her at Sheldon Oaks, Hampstead, London NW3.

Hope this helps,

Clarissa Blount-Pulverdart

THIRTY-THREE

Polly Slaughter knitted one, slip-stitched and started another row. The wool felt cosy and warm in her lap. She pondered a question she returned to often: if her name had been 'Love' would she have written romance? She came to her usual answer: no, she didn't think so. She'd just been lucky enough to be born with a name that fitted what she was good at – writing crime.

Fifty-something books, fifty-something million sold. Polly had done well for herself. She hadn't planned on retiring but the books had stopped coming. Why? Her readers would buy anything with her name on it. She could write a whodunnit in her sleep. Put a group of characters in a location, have a murder, the investigation begins, suspects accumulate, lead the audience in the direction of one, then hit them with a twist. Maybe the suspect gets arrested but another person dies. That usually does the trick. Then up the stakes, perhaps put the chief investigator in danger right before they reveal all. Wrap up your B and C plots, maybe a final twist, then have your investigator say they're leaving the game but hint that they'll always be ready for the next case, paving a path for the next book in the series.

But Polly had stumbled upon a new obsession: morphine. She'd had a hip operation a couple of years ago and lay in her private hospital room with her own button that topped her up with morphine whenever she wanted it. Polly had never taken drugs, but this stuff was delicious. She'd thought she'd led a good life – money and adulation, a family who loved her. Now she wondered if she'd wasted it, if the junkie on the park bench had had a better time than her.

Once she was out of hospital, Polly decided that continuing to feed her new enthusiasm for opiates on tap would be unhealthy and, crucially, could require an awful lot of life admin. For Polly Slaughter, getting in touch with Patricia Cornwell was easy but finding a reliable heroin dealer was a tougher ask. Instead, she'd managed to meet someone who gave her a steady supply of cannabis. A far lower risk of encountering the law or becoming the first winner of the Theakston Old Peculier Crime Novel of the Year Award to die with a belt strapped around their arm and a couple of milligrams of smack in their blood.

So she embraced her new weed-fuelled lifestyle but writing was a stretch. She couldn't get the words onto the page. Now she maintained a buzz, Winston Churchill-style, but the buzz was foggy, and she couldn't write with it. Knitting. That was the right activity for her. Most days she'd find a nice spot somewhere in the home and knit, letting a lovely, fuzzy wash of numbness fill her up.

Carol hadn't been to the library before and wasn't sure where it was. On the ground floor, by the lift, was a corridor she'd never ventured down. The walls were oak-panelled. This was the part of the building's interior that felt most like a stately home. Behind the first set of doors she came to she heard a high-pitched squeak that repeated itself once every second or so, as if a smoke alarm's battery was running low. Carol tentatively opened the big door to discover the noise was coming from the mouth of Belinda, who was sprawled on a snooker table with Marco on top of her. Her flushed face peered out from behind Marco's back.

'I think you'll find we have this room booked until five.'

Carol made her apologies and left them to it.

When she found the library behind the next door along the corridor, the only person in there was Polly, who sat in a brown leather chair, knitting, not talking to anyone. Sad, really. Three times her size, the chair swallowed Polly. She looked like an unsuspecting squirrel in the mouth of a giant bear.

The setting felt like the right place for an elderly thriller writer. It was the oldest-looking room in the building. Tall, dark oak bookshelves, table lamps with green shades – the sort of place an Agatha Christie murder might occur.

Carol sat in the armchair beside her and dropped a pile of books onto the coffee-table with a *thunk*. She started going through them one by one, reading out the titles.

'*Murder at the Nunnery, Murder at the Quarry, Murder at the Fun Fair, Murder at the Shoe Shop, Murder at the Allotment, Murder at the Department of Sanitation, Murder at the Chiropodist* . . . You've written an awful lot of books, Polly, but there's one missing – *Murder at the Retirement Home.*'

Polly looked at Carol with a contented smile. 'Everything all right, dear? You seem agitated.'

Carol was thrown. She'd come in hard but received a strangely placid reaction. Was this senility? Plough on regardless.

'You know a lot about murder, Polly . . .'

'Not as much as you do, dear.'

'I do,' said Carol. 'I know that only seven per cent of murders are committed by women.'

'Oh, yes?'

'Men, they'll kill anyone if you give them half a chance. I was the same, if I'm honest with myself. Bit of a tomboy, but women in general? Do you know who they're most likely to kill?'

'Let me think.' Polly paused, enjoying the quiz question. 'Their spouse?'

'That's right, Polly.'

Polly smiled. Carol continued: 'Their spouse or, and this is the key, *their ex-spouse.*'

Polly set her knitting on her lap.

'What are you knitting, Polly?'

'A scarf.'

'Who for?'

'A friend.'

'Do you mind if I take a look?'

Carol took a ball of yarn and looked at it closely.

'This wool, it's quite different, isn't it?' The wool came in quarter-inch-long bands of fluorescent yellow, blue and lime green. 'It's very loud, Polly.'

'I like the way it makes me feel when I'm knitting. I get lost in the colours. I suppose you might call it psychedelic.'

'It's very unusual, but, do you know, I think I've seen it somewhere before.'

Polly said nothing. Just looked at Carol with a rigid smile.

'On your ex-husband's dead body.'

Polly blinked, the accusation of murder shifting her out of whatever stupor she was in. Until now, though the two had hardly ever spoken, Carol had been surprised by how happily Polly had accepted the interrogation. Suddenly the mood was different.

'How strange.'

'It would make perfect sense if you were the one who killed him.'

Polly took a bite from a slice of cake in her handbag. Her hand shook.

'Would you like a bite dear?' Polly whispered. 'It's called a "hash" cake.' She must have caught Carol's quizzical look. 'At our age it's silly not to enjoy yourself, I think.' She leant in conspiratorially. 'I can get us some spice if you want. It's sort of like LSD but really packs a punch. I took a shower while I was on it once and I used a whole bar of soap. A whole bar of soap in one shower! I was just terrifically wired. I have a connection for the good stuff. I can hook you up if you like.'

Carol remembered their interaction by the lift on the day her secret had come out and the entire home had discovered her murderous past. She'd thought that Polly was a terrified old lady. Now she realised she had most likely been out of her mind on drugs.

'So you and Desmond were married, huh?'

'That was a very long time ago.'

'Why did you divorce?'

'He was a complicated man.' Polly took another nibble of her cake, wiped her hands with a napkin, then corrected herself: 'Actually, no. He was a very simple man. That was his problem. Only interested in simple pleasures. Like sex with other women. He got someone pregnant and that was my cue to leave.'

'Must have been difficult to see him here every day.'

Polly let out a genuine laugh. 'Ha! Difficult for *me*? You think I was still crying myself to sleep every night over Desmond? Half a century later? We were only married for a year. I got away quickly but stayed long enough for his job to inspire me into writing crime. That worked out rather nicely for me. Have you met his awful daughter? If I'd been enough of an idiot to stick around, she could have been mine!'

'I thought he got someone pregnant *before* you left?'

'No, that was somebody else. He managed to do it with some poor waitress when we were on our honeymoon and I was asleep in the hotel room. She travelled all the way to London to find us. She was holding a beautiful little baby girl and he wasn't interested. I'm not sure he ever saw that poor little girl ever again. And he didn't see me until we bumped into each other in the sauna here one day. Seeing his body at eighty made him a lot easier to resist, I can tell you.'

'Polly Slaughter?'

Polly looked up hazily, hearing another voice. 'Yes, dear?'

Carol turned.

'Oh, hello, Carol,' said DS Laura Welsh. 'What a surprise to see that you two are friends. Polly, I've come into some information that concerns you and I'd like you to come with me to the station to assist me with my enquiries, please.'

'Is it about Desmond being her ex-husband?' said Carol.

'No. What?' Laura failed to disguise that this was a completely new piece of information to her.

'Is it about her drug use?'

'No. What?'

'Ah, I see,' said Carol, lifting up the ball of yarn. 'It's about the fabric. That bright yarn she's holding is the fabric you found on Desmond's corpse, isn't it?'

Laura frowned, unable to stop herself nodding.

THIRTY-FOUR

Carol sat on her balcony, a puzzle book she couldn't turn her mind to on her lap. A duvet of dark cloud spanned the sky. It hadn't rained in weeks. People were out on the lawn playing croquet again. She picked up her binoculars to identify the participants.

Jim was there, as ever, directing the play. Geoffrey was standing on the periphery, no doubt uncomfortable at not being in charge. Margaret and Catherine were sitting on a bench, watching the action (though action was a generous word) and sharing a flask of tea.

Carol spotted an abandoned lawnmower. Even Tyler was joining in. Elisa came out and called his name angrily. He sulked over to her and they walked inside together. Poor lad, thought Carol. She noticed that the rope fence he'd been working on when she first arrived had never been finished. Perhaps there was a little room for improvement in his work ethic but Carol instinctively sided with those on the lowest rung of the ladder.

One of Carol's final murders had been that of her boss.

Authority had always rubbed her the wrong way. When her little sandwich business had ended, she'd needed work, so had applied for the job of secretary to a jeweller. He'd had a few branches around town, a few million in the bank, and was under the mistaken impression that it was all down to hard work, not luck. She could still smell his tobacco breath, feel his eyes on her young body when he asked her to do a twirl in his office. She'd known in that moment that he had to die but this time she'd do some planning first. This would be no spontaneous kill. She was coming to realise she had a talent, and talented people, whatever their skill, whether it was baking cakes or murder, deserved to be paid.

So, she tolerated him for a time. Ignored his hand on her bottom, laughed at his jokes, gained his trust, and slowly but surely moved his money into a different account.

Then, one Friday night, when he was planning to squeeze his fat frame into his Porsche and drive to his place on the coast, a place he insisted on calling his 'pad', she accompanied him to the pub and filled his drinks with sedative. On the Monday, she'd arrived at work to the news she had hoped for. Her boss was dead. When she looked back now, she was grateful that no one else had died. That had been a careless way for her to go about killing someone: he could easily have taken a few others with him. The recklessness of youth, she guessed. He and his car had slammed into a bridge and crumpled like accordions, and she, though no one else knew it, was a millionaire.

This was one of the murders she'd never been caught for, one that didn't count towards her official total of seven. As far as the world knew, it had never happened; sometimes your best work comes with no credit, but it was the murder that had paid for her place at Sheldon Oaks.

Carol looked out at the lawn again. Everyone was there, everyone but Polly, whose fate presumably lay in the hands of the Crown Prosecution Service. A home full of investigators but it had been Carol who had cracked the case. Ex-cricketers made the best umpires and ex-murderers made the best sleuths: it was only the professionals who truly understood the game. Polly's unmasking could lead to Carol's reintroduction to society. That was what she hoped. Maybe she'd join them in a minute, tell them the news.

But what if Polly didn't do it? Was a piece of fabric enough to convict someone? Why would Polly wait all that time to get her revenge on Desmond? The whole story was surely yet to be told. Maybe they'd all done it. Desmond was pushed, poisoned, strangled, bludgeoned. Maybe it was a case of death by a thousand or, more precisely, four murderers. Elisa could have messed with his medicine dose and poisoned him. Then Jim could have hit him on the head with a croquet mallet, before Tyler or Shep strangled him and Polly gave him a final hug, leaving the wool on his top, before pushing him off the edge.

But that wouldn't be much of a whodunnit, would it? Polly wouldn't like that one bit. What's the point of spending all this time on a mystery when there are no wrong answers? Who did it? They all did. Like a children's sports day when everyone gets a medal. No, that wouldn't do. There was only room for one person at the top of this particular podium and it was Polly.

Carol looked down at her crossword and finally took in a clue.

1 across. Smoothie company (eight letters).

This was one of those clues Carol could never get. All those years away and some things just escaped her. She didn't even know what a smoothie was. Was it something to do with skateboarding? A new genre of music?

She heard men's voices yelling and looked back to the lawn. Jim had his finger in Geoffrey's face. They were too old to be letting testosterone get the better of them, surely. Perhaps they had history. It occurred to her that she'd never considered Geoffrey as the possible murderer and that that had been an oversight.

A flash of lightning and then, a split second later, thunder. The heavens opened. The group headed indoors, none of them able to move quickly enough to avoid a soaking, and Carol was, in that moment at least, grateful not to be a part of the gang.

THIRTY-FIVE

Giles Temple walked out of the rain, down from the roof and straight into his office. He shook himself like a wet dog and let out a huge sigh. The steady hum of anxiety that dominated his life wouldn't budge. He scrolled through some TikTok videos. The algorithm was pushing him ways to be happy – exercise, vegetables, therapy, the ocean, a dog, sleep. Giles knew that none of them could cure his funk. Money. Money. Giles needed money. And until things had quietened down, his only reliable revenue stream was cut off.

He'd tried everything: making honey, installing a climbing wall. *Everything.* Recently, after afternoon sessions in Wetherspoons, he'd taken to calling up business associates and making threats. Stupid, he knew, but that was how panicked Giles was. A public-school boy, the weakest on the rugby team, playing the hard man. The cap didn't fit.

He caught a glimpse of himself in the reflection on his phone. He wasn't getting any younger.

There was a way out. He didn't want to take it but it was there. Someone had offered to buy the home. Until now, he'd resisted it. Sheldon Oaks was the Temple legacy. Letting it leave the family felt like a betrayal of his father. He'd disappointed him in life and now he'd be disappointing him in death.

But the offer was a life-raft, the only one he could see. Maybe Giles just had to accept that he was not an exceptional person, not in any way. Whatever he set his mind to, he was destined to fail because Giles Temple was a very average man. Below average, in fact. He was a schlub, a loser. But at least if he took the offer he'd be a loser with money.

He stared at his phone, his thumb hovering over the 'send' button. Sod it.

Okay you've twisted my arm. Let's do it.

Whoosh.

He sent messages to the people who needed to know and sat back. For the first time in months, his shoulders dropped.

Yes. It had been the right decision.

He took off his damp clothes, put on a dressing-gown and took the lift down to the basement. One last sauna to celebrate.

Giles didn't hear the lock turn on the sauna door. His eyes closed, he was enjoying the bliss of the end of his financial worries. Why had he wavered? Of course it was the right thing to do. Twenty minutes ago he'd been in despair. Now his confidence was already returning. Now that he was about to have some cash again, should he get back into business? Maybe open another restaurant? Of course he should! He was older and wiser now. He was Giles Temple, and Giles Temple – if you discounted everything he'd done in his life so far – could do anything he set his mind to.

When he felt his nose hairs start to burn he stood up, pulled down the handle and pushed. Time to get working on a new business plan.

But the door wouldn't move.

It felt like no one ever used the sauna but him. Another pointless facility, another waste of cash. He banged on the door, yelled until his throat hurt. In space, no one can hear you scream. The same could be said of a sauna at an old people's home. He might as well have been in a capsule, floating through the cosmos.

A sauna was a pleasant place to be, as long as you chose to be there. The second you wanted to leave but couldn't, it became an unbearable nightmare.

He knew he'd been murdered and, as death approached, he knew who'd done it. How could he have been so stupid?

Giles spent his final moments before passing out trying to remember the difference between a raisin, a sultana and a currant. What was a prune? Was it a dried plum? And what would they call Giles Temple, when they found his shrivelled corpse?

THIRTY-SIX

When the group moved indoors and went their separate ways, Catherine and Geoffrey found themselves taking the lift together, alone. Had he engineered it that way? Had they both? It had been that way in Catherine's university days. Something would be building with a boy and you'd just find yourselves, through an unsaid agreement, side by side.

Geoffrey opened his mouth to speak, paused, then let out the sentence that was on his mind.

'Catherine, would you like a cup of tea? In my flat? Or coffee?'

Catherine opened her mouth to speak but Geoffrey couldn't stop talking.

'If you don't want tea or coffee I don't have any wine but I do have some whisky, which I got for Christmas, although if you like ice with your whisky I'm not really an ice person so I don't have any in the fridge, I'm afraid. I think they sell ice in shops now. Would you like me to go and get you some ice from the shops?'

'A cup of tea would be lovely, thank you, Geoffrey.'

Geoffrey nodded and smiled. He looked nice when he smiled, thought Catherine. There was nothing conventionally attractive about him – the bags under his eyes were almost as big as his eyes themselves. But at Catherine's age she was beyond aesthetics. She could see behind his eyes, and behind his eyes Geoffrey looked . . . nice.

At Geoffrey's place, Catherine felt strangely at home. She recognised the clock on the wall as one she'd had in the eighties. Geoffrey talked at length about how a number of errors had been made in the electrical wiring of Sheldon Oaks. Switches were in the wrong places; problems were being stored up; the legacy of EU over-regulation hung over British buildings like a bad smell. Catherine found that, if you ignored everything he said, his voice was comforting. A man's voice. Even if they were talking complete rubbish, there was a security, she thought, in the certainty that men projected.

Her phone pinged with a text and she took it from her handbag. Margaret: *The police have arrested Polly Slaughter for Desmond's murder! lol*

And then another text came: *Sorry ive just remembered my££ nephew told me lol doesn't mean lots of love. Not lol. Meet in the bistro in ten minutes???send text£*

Catherine relayed the news to Geoffrey.

'Polly Slaughter, eh?'

'Margaret wants to meet in the bistro. I suppose she wants to discuss what comes next.'

'Well, I'd imagine if Polly's charged she'll get out on bail pending a trial,' said Geoffrey. 'Although considering that would send her back here, to the scene of the crime, perhaps they'll keep her on remand. Gosh. Polly Slaughter – on remand!'

'I think Margaret means what comes next with us. And our investigation.'

'Right,' said Geoffrey. 'I see. Well, I'm sure there's a lot to be looked into. How she did it. Why. Are there any holes in their case? Are we sure they have the right man? Woman. Right woman.'

'Mmm.'

They sat in a beat of silence, looking into each other's eyes.

'Catherine, how would you feel about *not* going down to meet Margaret?'

Catherine shrugged. 'I don't have to.'

'Why don't you stay here with me and watch *The World at War*? I have the whole series on DVD. All twenty-six episodes. Obviously, I'm not suggesting that we . . .'

'That would be lovely.'

And so they sat on Geoffrey's sofa and watched episode one, which was about the rise of the Nazis. Geoffrey couldn't stop himself chipping in with his own analysis.

'I don't know if Drexler gets enough credit. There's a lot of Hitler and Göring, you know, but Drexler did an awful lot of the ground work for them in the early years. You understand, when I say credit, I don't mean – I'm not *pro-Nazi* – I happen to think, and you can quote me on this, I happen to think that the Nazis were dreadful. Absolutely dreadful.'

'I understand,' said Catherine, resting her head on his shoulder. And she did understand. Geoffrey Standing was a lovely man who just needed to feel loved. Maybe she could do that for him. She couldn't see his face, but she felt sure that Geoffrey was happy to have her body so close to his.

After a while, sometime around the annexation of Czechoslovakia, Geoffrey nodded off. Catherine, who hadn't been paying much attention to the programme, took out her phone. Margaret had replied to Catherine's message asking to meet tomorrow instead with a simple – or was it a curt? – *Ok*. Was this really happening? Were she and Geoffrey about to pair off and leave Margaret like the gooseberry? No. Catherine couldn't let that happen. Perhaps, now that Polly was to be put away, Carol would be reintegrated. Although Catherine had to wonder just how comfortable she really was being friends with the author of those diaries.

She fiddled around on her phone. An email had arrived from Nigel. Nigel? She hated herself for feeling a flutter of nerves. Nothing could have prepared her for what the email contained.

Dearest Catherine,

I do hope we can be grown-ups about this. I've told the children and they're all delighted for Emily and me. The long and the short of it is that we're getting married. I suggested inviting you but Emily, understandably, didn't want competition in the room. Not that, beautiful as you are, anyone could be competition for Emily, the love of my life. Seeing as this leaves you the only person in England who's free on that particular weekend, how would you feel about looking after our dogs?

Best wishes,

Nigel

Catherine threw her phone across the room.

Geoffrey was still asleep but Catherine had to do something with her instant rage. She needed somewhere to put it.

'Catherine?' Geoffrey had woken up to find her hand on his crotch. He looked at her, stunned but overjoyed. 'I ... I really ... Catherine, I'm afraid I need a little medical assistance. I have some pills in the bathroom.'

'Take one. Now.'

Catherine and Geoffrey carried out her revenge sex on his bed. The television still on, they could hear a detailed description of the Saar Offensive coming from the living room.

Catherine put her back into it, like digging the garden, hoping the physical exertion would take her mind off the news. But it couldn't. Maybe one day she could fall in love with Geoffrey, but it could never be the same. She was too old; he was too old. The older you got, the more distinct you got. You became who you were. She could never give herself to another man like she had with Nigel.

Catherine was heartbroken.

No. That wouldn't do. Catherine needed to get out of her head and into her body. All that swimming, all that yoga, what was it for, if not for this? She pushed herself to her limits, stretching them both into a position never before performed by a couple with their combined age.

Living in central London for years, as she had, Catherine was familiar with the mating call of foxes. You'd often hear it at night as they prowled the bins – an ugly, terrifying shriek. For the first time in her life, Catherine now heard that sound coming out of the mouth of a human.

'Argh! Aaaaargh! Jesus H bloody Christ! I think I might have pulled my calf!' rasped Geoffrey.

Catherine rolled off him and they stared at the ceiling.

'I'm sorry, Catherine. That was terrific, it really was. I'm just a little out of practice.'

'That's all right, Geoffrey. I got a little carried away. Why don't you see if you can sleep it off?' said Catherine.

Catherine felt guilty. She'd used Geoffrey's body as a repository for her anger and it hadn't worked. She'd given the poor man an injury but the rage hadn't faded. Her eyes narrowed. There was only one person who could help her now: Carol.

THIRTY-SEVEN

Carol was on her fourth episode of *Women Who Kill*. Or perhaps her fifth? You used to have to wait a week for a new episode of your favourite TV programme. Now, if you didn't move, they just kept coming. She couldn't sit there all day. Maybe she'd get up and try out one of the many Sheldon Oaks facilities she'd never bothered with. Just one more episode.

A knock at the door startled her. Something about the sound suggested the person on the other side was in a rush. This was no jaunty playful knock, rather the knock of a person who wanted something. Now. Carol opened the door, slowly.

'I need you to tell me how to kill someone.'

Carol grabbed Catherine's arm and pulled her into the flat, checking the corridor was empty before closing the door.

'Tea?'

'No, thank you.'

'Take a seat.'

They sat at Carol's round glass kitchen table. It felt odd not to have a drink of some kind, just to sit there beverage-free, like it was a job interview, but Catherine clearly wasn't in the mood for distractions.

'You didn't fancy the *Mamma Mia* matinee outing, then?' said Carol. 'I saw them head off in the minibus.'

'Can't stand musicals,' said Catherine.

They had a lot in common, thought Carol. 'Have you heard about Polly?'

'Yes. Who would have thought? Carol, I'm sorry about all the—'

'It's fine,' said Carol. 'I can see why I was your suspect. I hope we can be—'

'Friends again? Of course.'

Carol took a breath and broached the subject at hand. 'So you want to . . .'

'Kill somebody, yes.' Catherine stretched the tension from her arms, hearing herself say the words. 'My ex-husband, Nigel. He's getting remarried and – oh, God, I'm such a cliché – Carol, he *has* to die. I just can't go about my day knowing that he's out there living and breathing and going about his. Carol, there's no way I can explain it, he's just . . . he's just such a . . . he's just such a wally.'

Carol looked at Catherine. She'd known there had to be more than met the eye. Nobody's perfect. Everyone fantasises about murder, everyone, but few go so far as to consult a specialist. 'How do you want to do it?'

'I was hoping you might be able to help me with that. I mean, I'll carry out the . . .' Catherine swallowed '. . . *murder*, but I'd appreciate some guidance. I don't want to get caught. I just want him eliminated. I don't have a gun. Do you have a gun?'

'Never had one, Catherine, no. Too noisy, don't you think? Tricky to get hold of, tricky to get rid of. Also, they've always seemed to me like they're no fun. Too easy. One click and they're dead. It's like shopping online. I find it soulless. If you're going to go to all that fuss, why not make a day of it?'

Carol felt flattered to have been consulted and it was a pleasure to speak on a subject she knew so much about. She'd had admirers but rarely did anyone ask her about the nuts and bolts. No one ever asks musicians about the actual music, do they?

Catherine picked up a pen from Carol's table and started fidgeting with it. 'Okay, what would you suggest?'

People always wanted to know about the things that surrounded murder, but here was someone actually asking her what chords to play.

'Right. What would I suggest? Um . . .' Carol leant back and pondered her favourite topic. 'He doesn't have a boat, does he?'

Catherine shook her head.

'That's a shame. I always wanted to do something on a boat. There's a glamour to that, don't you think? Drown him, cut him up in the motor, leave him to the eels.'

'I was thinking something more . . .'

'You just want to get the job done, don't you, Catherine? Something simple.'

Catherine nodded.

'Is he on any drugs? Prescription, I mean.'

'A few tablets. This and that.'

'That's a pretty easy one. Fiddle with his pills. But you'd need access to his medicine cabinet. Is that . . .?'

'Not easy, no.'

'Mmm. But you're a doctor. You could get hold of something.'

'I suppose so.'

'Traceable, though,' said Carol, thinking it through. She was in her element. 'Did you ever watch the ... What are they called? Looney Tunes? Wile E. Coyote. I wonder if anyone's ever tried that. Dropping a weight on someone from a great height.'

'Didn't it always land on him?'

'Good point. Good point. Sorry, here I am trying to be original and you just want your husband dead. We're not trying to make *Sgt. Pepper's* here, are we? Right, how did Desmond go? Poisoned, strangled and pushed.'

'And bludgeoned,' chipped in Catherine.

'Oh, yes, bludgeoned. That's not a bad list. All pretty tried and tested. How easy is it for you to see him? Are you on friendly terms?'

Catherine deadpanned Carol. 'He thinks we are.'

'Good.'

'Will you be seeing him soon, for any reason?'

'Our grandson's eighteenth. We're all going for a big restaurant dinner, somewhere in London. It's in a couple of weeks.'

'Perfect. Well, I mean, Catherine, I do keep finding myself going back to poison. That gives us enough time to get some without it tracing back to you. How many people will there be there?'

'At least thirty.'

'Nice. Lots of suspects. No one will ever imagine it could have been Grandma. And what this gives you is the opportunity to watch him die. Catherine, trust me on this, if you're only going to do one murder, make sure you see them die. Too many of mine died out of sight. There's nothing quite like watching the results of your own hard work.'

Catherine's eyes became glassy. Her breath juddered as she inhaled and went back to fiddling with the pen.

Carol spoke softly. 'Or you could always not murder him.'

'You probably think I'm a terrible wimp.'

'Not at all.'

'It's just . . . in front of all our children.'

'Do you know the problem with murder?' said Carol.

Catherine looked up from the pen.

'I had a friend in prison. We used to say it's like Chinese food. It fills you up but only for an hour or so. Then you want more. Whatever it is, whatever the feelings are that make you want to kill someone, when you've killed them, those feelings don't go away.' Carol spoke tenderly. 'What's your grandson's name?'

Catherine grew a small smile. 'Finn.'

'They give them such funny names, don't they, the parents now?'

Catherine nodded, rubbing her nose with the back of her hand. 'Don't get me started. His sister's called Oslo. They're very smart, though. You should see Finn. He's got all this energy. Brilliant at sport. Plays cricket with his right hand, plays tennis with his left, it's incredible. Off to university in September to do something ridiculous like American Studies. We're both . . .' Catherine's voice trembled '. . . we're both so proud.'

Carol stared into the middle distance for a moment. 'You still love him, don't you?'

Catherine nodded.

Had Carol ever been in love? She wasn't sure that she had. Not like this.

'Why don't you just knock off the new woman?'

Catherine laughed. 'Oh, not much point. I'm sure she won't be around for long. She's nothing more than Anne Boleyn in a Toyota Yaris. It's him I'm angry with.'

'How do you know what car he drives?' asked Carol.

'Oh, some people put everything on Facebook, don't they? Don't you snoop on your exes?'

Carol contemplated the question. 'I haven't had a lover in nearly forty years.'

'Sorry.'

Carol stood up. 'Let's sweat it out.'

Catherine looked at her, puzzled.

'The sauna. Do you use it?'

'Now and again,' said Catherine.

'I've not been there yet. Never been in a sauna. Can't really see the point, if I'm honest. I mean, I've been in a hot room. I've been on the tube in summer. Is it the same as that?'

Catherine pondered the question. 'Well, you wear a swimming costume so not *exactly* the same. And the air is a lot purer.'

'You should try everything once, right?' said Carol.

'Except murder.'

'Yeah, except that.'

THIRTY-EIGHT

Carol arrived in the basement corridor first. Catherine had suggested that she wear a swimming costume and dressing-gown but Carol had neither (there wasn't much use for swimming costumes in prison), so she was in her bra and knickers with an anorak over the top. Thank God she hadn't seen anyone.

In front of the lift doors there was a small gym. Carol peered inside. Empty. She'd never seen a proper gym before. In the prison yard there'd been an area with some weights where the Aryan Sisterhood hung out, but she'd avoided it. Early on, she'd had to make a choice. Which group would she associate herself with for protection? Everyone needed a tribe. In the end she'd opted for the crossword club over white supremacy. Better biscuits.

'I feel like a flasher,' she said to Catherine, who'd arrived in a white towelling dressing-gown, her hair neatly tied back.

'Don't worry. You look fine. It's this way.'

Catherine led her down the corridor and turned right. The sauna door was wooden with a small porthole window.

'That's strange. It's locked.' Catherine pushed the door again then looked through the window. 'Oh, Jesus.' She stood back and covered her mouth.

Carol went to the window. Inside a naked man was sprawled on the floor, face down.

'I've seen enough dead bodies,' said Catherine. 'That is a corpse.'

Carol knew Catherine was right. They were two very different people but that was one thing they shared: a familiarity with the dead. 'We need to get in there,' she said.

'Carol, I'm not really in the mood for a sauna any more, if I'm honest. We should just tell somebody at Reception.'

'The door's locked,' said Carol.

'I'm sure they'll have a key.'

'Think about it,' said Carol. 'Why would that man lock himself in there? It's been locked from the outside. This is murder.'

Catherine's face slackened, the truth dawning on her. 'Then we should call the police,' she said.

'But this means that maybe Polly didn't kill Desmond. Surely it's the same murderer. Don't you think? I mean, this place isn't crawling with murderers, is it?'

'Apart from you.'

'Apart from me, yes.' Carol laughed. 'You see what I'm saying, though, yes? Don't you want to solve the case?'

Catherine hardened. 'More than anything.'

'We get the police involved, we go and tell Reception, it'll get messy. We'll be in the dark. You know who they'll turn their sights on again, don't you? Me. I *have* to solve this case to clear my name. Do you trust me?'

Catherine paused, then nodded.

'Thank you. You were a forensic scientist, yes?'

Catherine nodded again.

'Then let's do a little autopsy.'

'We could get into an awful lot of trouble,' said Catherine.

'We need to get in there. Turn away.'

'What?'

'Just look away for a second.' Carol stuffed her hand into her chest.

Catherine turned away. She spoke to the wall: 'Carol, may I ask what you're doing?'

'I'm getting the wire out of my bra.'

'Why?'

'Why do you think? Stupid bloody thing.' Carol yanked at it, then fed the wire through. 'You can turn back now.' Carol held up the wire, pleased with herself. 'That bra was fighting a losing battle anyway.' She put the wire into the lock.

'Carol, I'm not sure this is going to . . . Oh, you've done it.'

Carol opened the door, smugly turning to Catherine. 'It's a sauna, not a bank vault.'

The heat hit them like an oven. Catherine knelt down and put her fingers to the body's neck, checking his pulse. 'He's cooked.'

'That's not a resident, is it?' said Carol. 'Look at his bum. That is a young man's bum.'

Catherine couldn't help but smirk.

'Not that I'm particularly interested in young men's bums,' said Carol.

'You're sweating,' said Catherine.

'Shut up. Who is it? We should turn him over.'

Carol got down beside Catherine and they rolled the body over.

'Giles,' said Catherine.

Carol let out a little shriek.

'You're not surprised, are you?' said Catherine. 'I'd assumed it was Giles.'

'No, it's his pubic hair. He's hardly got any.'

'Yes, I'm told they do that now,' said Catherine. 'All the young men, they trim it. Very strange.'

'Sick, if you ask me,' said Carol.

The two women stared at Giles's privates, as if they were a particularly rude piece of graffiti.

'I quite agree,' said Catherine.

THIRTY-NINE

The room was airy, the wooden floor shiny and new. It felt unused. They were underground, there were no windows, and the bright overhead lights buzzed in the quiet. On the wall there was a picture of Bruce Lee and some banal motivational quotes, probably straight from Google:

The body achieves what the mind believes.

Don't dream of winning.
Train for it.

And worst of all:

Nothing is impossible.
The word itself says I'm possible.

Carol had to remind herself that she was in an old people's home, the martial-arts studio of an old people's home, but an old people's home nonetheless. Some things *were* impossible:

each resident was reminded of it every day. Touching your toes, for example. Getting out of bed without groaning, or watching a whole film without needing the toilet. In the corner she noticed a sunken trampoline. *A trampoline.* Was Giles Temple the worst businessman of all time? Shep was surely his only competition. For the first time, it occurred to her that they were near enough the same person – two men of low IQ and high advantage, both frittering away their fortuitous starts in life.

They heard a gentle knock and saw Margaret's face pressed against the door's window, with Geoffrey hovering behind. Carol let them in, suddenly very aware that she was still in bra, knickers and an anorak. Luckily there were bigger distractions at play. Margaret immediately spotted the body on the floor.

'That's Giles Temple,' she said.

'Correct,' said Carol.

'And he's dead,' said Geoffrey.

'Correct,' said Catherine. 'I'm about to carry out an autopsy. We thought you two might like to join us.'

Catherine and Carol were standing next to the corpse, almost proud, like two sisters who'd just completed a Lego set. Margaret took a bite from a croissant, then slowly lowered it back into her handbag.

'We found him in the sauna,' said Carol. 'He was locked in there. It had to have been locked from the outside. Somebody has murdered him.'

'But ... how did you, why, I don't understand ... How is he in here?'

'We dragged him,' said Carol. 'Catherine's very fit, as you know, and I'm very strong.'

'But . . . now, hang on. Has it occurred to anyone that this means Polly is not the murderer?'

'Yes, Geoffrey,' said Carol and Catherine, groaning in unison. 'We're well ahead of you there.'

'And if Polly is not the murderer, then,' Geoffrey's arm extended and slowly rose, his finger directing itself at Carol, 'Carol . . .'

'Oh, shut up, Geoffrey,' said Carol. 'If you don't stop accusing me of murder I'm going to kill you, I really am.'

'She didn't do it, Geoffrey,' said Catherine. 'I'm sure of it.'

'You're asking me to trust your hunch.'

'An hour or two ago I was determined to kill my ex-husband. Long story. He's a wally. I went to Carol and asked her how to do it. She talked me out of it. She told me how killing isn't worth it, how it doesn't fill the hole. I'm telling you now, Carol may have been a murderer, but she isn't one any more.'

Carol should have taken it as a compliment, really, but she couldn't help feeling a pang of sadness at the loss of her identity. If she wasn't a murderer, what was she? Still, nice of her friend to stand up for her, and Catherine's little speech appeared to have won over Geoffrey and Margaret.

Catherine addressed Geoffrey. 'Now, we're going to examine the body. Would you care to assist us?' she said, then hit him with the sentence he'd waited his entire life to hear: 'We would all very much value your expertise.'

Geoffrey puffed out his chest and happily plodded over to Catherine, Carol and the corpse.

'Is nobody a little worried that we might be found?' said Margaret. 'It's been a while since I practised law but I can assure you this is all very illegal.'

'Do you hear anyone? No one's been in this room for months. Margaret, please don't spoil our fun,' pleaded Carol, immediately taking Margaret back to when she, as a teenage Goody Two Shoes, discovered her school mates smoking out of the dormitory window after bedtime. That time she'd ignored them, told the matron and been an outcast for the rest of her school life. She wouldn't make the same mistake again.

'No, no, you go ahead. Carry on with the – uh – impromptu autopsy.'

Carol watched Catherine adjust herself and transition into a professional mode. She immediately looked twenty years younger. Her friend held up Giles's arm. 'I think we're looking at somewhere between twelve and twenty-four hours since death. Decomposition hasn't started just yet, but we're in the final stages of rigor mortis.'

'Yes, yes, I concur, I concur,' said Geoffrey, enthusiastically nodding along.

'Sorry, would anyone mind if I covered his willy?' said Margaret. 'I'm just finding it difficult to concentrate.'

'Go ahead,' said Catherine.

Margaret took a hankie from her bag and delicately placed it over the offending genitalia, holding back her head as if she was dealing with a dog turd. 'When did you cut off his pubic hair?' she asked. 'Just before we got here? I presume it's part of the process?'

'Oh, no,' said Carol. 'He, uh, came like that.'

'Ah,' said Margaret, nodding. 'So the murderer is some kind of sex maniac.'

'No, no,' said Catherine. 'It's a modern trend. He likely did it to himself. Called manscaping, I believe.'

'You a manscaper, Geoffrey?' asked Carol, and the three ladies giggled, Catherine hiding her face from the blushing Geoffrey.

'If it is, as you say, Catherine, a modern trend, then for now I'm going to class the pubic-hair length as not, in and of itself, suspicious.'

'Thank you, Geoffrey,' said Catherine, moving things along. She inspected Giles Temple's face. 'Sunken eyes, dark circling around here,' she said, as if dictating notes to an assistant. 'The skin is very dry. This is all consistent with terminal dehydration.'

'Poor man,' said Margaret.

Carol looked at the corpse properly for the first time and couldn't help but empathise. What a horrible way to die. Locked in an oven of your own making, gasping for air. To die in a sauna was a shame; to die in a sauna that you had personally designed and paid for was a bitch. Did he see his executioner or did he suffer in ignorance? She had to admire the killer and their imagination. Locking someone in their own sauna was a method that had never occurred to her. This was a murderer with a sadistic streak that matched her own. Maybe there was no rhyme or reason and looking for motives was a nonsense. This could be a new serial killer, taking up Carol's old hobby. If so, they were all at risk.

'The body loses water, the blood becomes thicker,

circulation decreases. I think he most likely suffered multiple organ failure,' said Catherine. 'If we were somewhere else and I had all my tools I might cut him open.'

'We wouldn't want to make a mess on the floor,' said Carol. 'It's very hard to get blood out of wood tiling. It gets stuck in the grooves.' She felt the other three looking at her. 'I'm sorry. It just is.'

'Catherine, I don't think I can bend down to get a proper look,' said Geoffrey. 'Is that a tattoo on his arm?'

'Oh, yes.'

Carol moved around the body for a better look. On Giles's bicep she saw a coat of arms with some Latin. Below the Latin was another word in a different font. 'What does that say?' she asked.

'Waynflete,' said Catherine.

'What's that?' asked Carol.

'Is it a service station?' said Geoffrey. 'No, I'm thinking of Fleet. Great services, it has to be said, but I don't think I'd be getting a tattoo. Could be a rock band or something. Maybe a cult he was in. Any mileage in that?'

'You're not far off,' said Margaret. 'It's a house.'

'A house?' said Catherine.

'At Eton. The boarders are divided into houses. Waynflete is one of them.'

Carol clenched at the mention of the place. She'd never considered herself a class warrior, live and let live, 'Some of my greatest friends are poshos' and all that – but something about that particular school rubbed her up the wrong way. She'd seen a TV documentary once and the juxtaposition of some of the most bully-able children she'd ever seen and their impenetrable confidence had made her a little sick in her mouth.

'How do you know that?' asked Catherine. 'I thought they only accepted boys at Eton.'

'I was in cabinet. You'd think they were all still at Eton from the way half of them banged on about it,' said Margaret.

'Desmond's son-in-law went to Eton. Calls himself Shep. They look about the same age. Could have been school mates,' said Carol.

'Or enemies,' said Catherine.

'Let's assume Giles went there,' said Geoffrey. 'Very well connected, you'd expect. Would be interesting to know who he's been in touch with. Could give us some clues. How this connects to Desmond, I don't know.'

'I have Giles's phone,' said Carol, holding it up. 'It was in his dressing-gown pocket.' She clicked a button on the side and looked at it. 'It seems to be working again. It had overheated when we found him.'

'You won't get in there without a pin,' said Geoffrey.

'Isn't it one two three four?' said Margaret. 'I thought everyone's was.' Carol could see Margaret feel the others looking at her. 'Not that *mine* is. Mine's much more complicated than that.'

Carol leant over Giles's body and held the phone towards his face.

'What are you doing?' asked Margaret.

'Face ID. Catherine, would you mind holding open his eyes?'

Clocking on, Catherine peeled open Giles's eyes. Margaret's face scrunched up in distaste.

Carol looked at the phone. 'I'm in.'

They all watched in anticipation as Carol fiddled around with Giles's phone.

'I can help you with that, if you like, Carol,' said Geoffrey. 'I got my first cellular phone in the early nineties, so I'm pretty *au fait* with the way they work.'

Carol made a noise. 'Huh.'

'What?' said Margaret.

'The last person he called was Shep. Yesterday morning.'

'Then we need to speak to Shep,' said Catherine.

Carol, Geoffrey and Margaret headed for the door with purpose.

'Hang on!' said Catherine. 'What do we do with the body?'

Catherine was so engaged, so full of life. Carol felt proud: her mind was no longer on her ex-husband. All it had taken was for a murder to happen and they hadn't even had to do the killing. Death could be such a wonderful palate-cleanser.

'Right,' said Carol. 'I suppose we put him back in the sauna so someone else can find him?'

It was agreed that they should all do their bit. This was a joint operation. Carol and Catherine took the arms, Geoffrey and Margaret the legs. The four retirees shuffled along the corridor with their corpse like it was a sofa.

Geoffrey led the way with unhelpful but constant instructions. 'Pivot! No, this way, that's it, pivot, okay, now rotate fifteen degrees. Ow, ow, my bloody calf, ow!'

'Geoffrey, sssh!' said Carol.

'What?' said Catherine.

Carol whispered, 'Did I just hear someone?'

The answer came immediately. Elisa came around the corridor and dropped her bags of shopping in shock. Something smashed. Carol tried to identify an old and familiar smell. Worcester sauce? They froze, caught red-handed with the dead body of Giles Temple. Elisa looked at them, they at her.

'Does this mean karaoke night is cancelled this week?' said Margaret.

FORTY

They'd been quiet for a while now, each thinking about the series of events that had led them from their luxury retirement home to a police cell. It was turning into some kind of community outreach scheme, with every resident getting their chance to spend a day in the slammer. Geoffrey lay on the floor for the good of his back. When he'd complained about the discomfort of the seating, Margaret had pointed out that higher taxes in exchange for more pleasant cells had never been a vote winner.

'Correct me if I'm wrong, Geoffrey, but wouldn't they usually separate us?' asked Margaret. 'So that we don't collude, concoct our story or what-have-you?'

'They may be low on cells,' said Geoffrey.

Carol stewed. All this had done was stall her and her investigation. Perhaps she shouldn't have involved the others, just done it herself, like the lone wolf she'd always been. But now that she'd found herself a pack, she didn't want to lose it.

She could see the others were fixated on Shep. It made sense. He'd stood to gain from Desmond's death, which meant he had a motive. And now there was reason to believe he'd had a long-standing association with Giles. She couldn't confirm it while they were in this wretched cell but it appeared likely that they'd gone to school together. Twenty-five years or so was more than enough time for him to build a grudge. Perhaps a business arrangement had gone wrong. Here were two men who dealt, exclusively it seemed, in failed business arrangements. What might this particular arrangement have been? The marijuana cakes in Desmond's room – could that have been an enterprise the three of them, Giles, Shep and Desmond, were running together? And now Shep was taking control? But were marijuana cakes really that profitable? Enough to kill for?

Carol had other ideas. Something Polly had said had been on her mind. There were avenues that needed pursuing, people who needed to be questioned, histories that needed to be explored. Margaret could help with that, if Carol could persuade her to take a little day trip. They'd be going nowhere as long as they were in the hands of the police ...

Carol's heart sank at a familiar sound: the opening of a cell door.

'All right, Golden Girls,' said DS Welsh. 'Come with me.'

Laura Welsh looked at the four of them and tried not to laugh. The four retirees were squashed together on one side of the table in Interview Room Two. The light was harsh. Behind them, paint was starting to peel off the wall. Margaret, Catherine and Geoffrey looked embarrassed, their eyes darting nervously around the room. The dead-eyed Carol stared straight ahead.

What a funny sight they had been. Especially Catherine in her swimming cossie and Carol, apparently dressed as a cartoon stripper. She'd allowed them ten minutes to change into something more dignified before she took them to the station.

That must have caused a stir at Sheldon Oaks. Four respectable-looking pensioners being bundled into a cop car and shipped to the nick – that would have got curtains twitching.

'This is serious stuff, you know. You moved a dead body.'

Geoffrey held up a finger. 'Ah. But can you prove that in a court of law?'

'I think you're forgetting that Margaret relived the whole story in the car on the way over here,' deadpanned Laura. 'I recorded it on my phone. You were all laughing.'

'We didn't do it! We didn't kill him!' said Catherine.

Laura spoke softly. 'I know you didn't.'

'How?' asked Carol.

'Call it a hunch. You're busybodies, not killers.'

'I'm a killer,' said Carol, offended. 'And what makes you think these three don't have it in them? Don't underestimate us, Laura. Geoffrey's got a temper – I've seen it. Catherine asked me to help her kill her ex-husband earlier on today, and Margaret, well, she's an ex-politician – she's capable of anything.'

Catherine butted in: 'Carol, I'm not sure you're—'

'I just think it stinks,' said Carol. 'People look at us and think we're just sitting around in nappies doing jigsaws. We're not a hundred, you know! We've got get-up-and-go! Geoffrey and Catherine shagged yesterday!'

Margaret spat out her tea.

'You should have heard some of the things they were doing. Really athletic stuff, the way Catherine describes it. Geoffrey sprained his calf! You think they don't have it in them to lock a wimp like Giles Temple in a sauna?'

Laura stopped drawing a cobweb in the corner of her notepad and put down her pen. 'I apologise if I've offended you. You are all very capable killers, I don't doubt it. But you're also all very bright. I just don't think you're stupid enough to walk around with the man you just killed in the middle of the day.'

Carol paused, relenting. 'All right, well, I see what you're getting at there, yes. I just don't want you looking at us and thinking, Oh, they're old, they could never be murderers.'

Margaret gently placed her hand on Carol's arm. 'Carol, as the only qualified lawyer in the room, may I suggest that you stop talking for a moment?'

Carol folded her arms.

'You've all been investigating Desmond's death, am I right?' said Laura.

They all nodded.

'Which I assume means you've accumulated some evidence.'

'A little,' said Catherine.

'You've most likely noticed we brought Polly in yesterday, and I'm sure it hasn't escaped your attention that, as there's been another murder while Polly was in custody, things are now kind of tricky for us.'

'You've got the wrong woman,' said Geoffrey.

'So it would seem.'

'Then what now?' said Catherine.

'Tell me everything you know and I'll let you go.'

Margaret opened her mouth but Carol spoke first. 'Hang on. Where's DCI Beattie?'

'Otherwise engaged.'

'Otherwise engaged?' said Carol. 'You've not told him, have you? He's off duty and you've thought to yourself how nice it would be to get this done on your own. Leyton Orient are playing at home today, aren't they? That's right. He's watching the football, so you thought you'd take advantage. Big case, this. Make the arrest yourself and you'll go up a few rungs, yes? I would have thought so. Desmond was a legend round here, wasn't he? For the wrong reasons? Maybe Beattie's been acting funny, too scared to delve into areas he shouldn't, but you're keen. You want to know *everything*.'

Laura was still, letting Carol do the talking.

'I think we're your best hope, Laura. Me, her, her and him. Four – what did you call us? – busybodies? Four busybodies who happen to be very good at it, on the inside. We're no good to you in here. If we tell you what we know, it'll get messy. Bob'll come back to work, you'll have to keep him informed, there'll be paperwork, rules, warrants probably.' Carol spoke softly, her head tilted. 'Why don't you let us do our job?'

'It's not your job. It's mine.'

'And how's that going? You've arrested two people for the murder and neither of them did it. Now you've brought me back in and added another three. It's like you're trying to assemble the world's worst prison football team.'

Laura pursed her lips.

'Let us out,' said Carol. 'We'll look where we need to look, find what we need to find, and once we've figured out who the murderer is, I'll invite you to the dénouement and you can make the arrest.'

'Dénouement?'

'I'm sure Polly can tell you about it when you release her in a minute. It's the bit at the end of the story when you find out who the killer is and everything gets wrapped up. Let us out and I promise it'll be along very soon.'

'Oh, hello, Polly,' said Carol. 'Fancy seeing you here.'

A dazed Polly had joined them in the police-station reception area.

'Hello,' said Polly, sitting down next to Carol on an ugly black pleather couch.

Laura, whose face was starting to betray her irritation, told them a taxi would be along for them in a moment.

'Probably best to get an XL,' said Geoffrey. 'There's one, two, three, four, five of us.'

Laura stared at them, silently doing her own head count, then disappeared, muttering under her breath.

Carol thought for a moment then asked Polly a question. 'Your honeymoon, Polly? Where was it?'

'Portugal.'

'Do you remember where in Portugal?'

Polly looked to the ceiling in search of the name. 'It was fifty years ago. Fedda . . . Ferra . . .?'

'Ferragudo?'

'You've been?'

'No,' said Carol. 'Sadly not.'

Laura came out of a back room.

'Taxi's here.' The tired detective opened the back door to the station and the five started to make their way down the ramp and into the car park. 'Carol.'

Carol turned. Laura was giving her the curly finger. 'Yes?'

Laura spoke quietly and firmly: 'I haven't ruled you out yet. If this goes tits up, if you let me down in any way, I will make sure you're back in prison before your feet touch the ground. I'll have to go and check but I'm pretty sure conducting an amateur autopsy counts as breaking your parole.'

Carol looked her in the eyes and gave her a nod. The message had been received. 'I'd better go and catch the killer then, hadn't I?'

Carol caught up with the others and sidled next to Margaret. 'Margaret, I wonder if you could do me a favour?'

FORTY-ONE

Carol and Margaret left Westminster tube station and took a stroll past Big Ben. Carol was tired after spending half the night on her computer, tying leads together, getting in touch with some old friends, doing a little online snooping. Today's sleuthing came in the form of a field trip and – if everything went to plan – this would be the last day of the investigation.

Before departing, Carol had taken a walk in the Sheldon Oaks gardens on her own. First, she had some measuring to do. The results were as she suspected.

How lucky she was to live there. She'd tried to remember the names of the flowers Margaret had told her. Lupines, monkshood, pink dahlias. Looking at the flowerbed closely, she noticed that a clump of flowers was missing. Not everything was perfect.

Margaret met her by the building's entrance and they'd taken the short walk to Hampstead tube station, Carol's first trip on the Underground this century. On the tube she remembered, people's faces were hidden behind giant newspapers. Now they all stared at their phones. The upholstery hadn't changed, exactly the same patterns. She asked Margaret who told her that, yes, the Bakerloo did still smell a bit eggy.

Above ground, everywhere they looked were Pret A Mangers and cyclists. This wasn't their London any more. Red phone boxes with prostitutes' cards in them, IRA bomb warnings, every room filled with a fog of cigarette smoke, clothes that always smelt of fags – that was their era. Things had moved on. Whether that was for the better was not for them to say.

They made their way past Parliament Green. There was a small collection of media tents, TV lighting rigs, young people in suits looking at their phones, some politician being interviewed on camera.

'Do you miss it?'

'That?' said Margaret. 'Not in the slightest. This is much more fun.'

Margaret hadn't been in the neighbourhood for a few months. The last time, she'd popped into the House of Lords to show her face, listened to a debate and had lunch in one of Parliament's dining rooms. Everyone had seemed so old. The lords, all nearing death, decades past their last cogent thought, as they sat in the chamber, blankets on their laps, bellies full of state-subsidised sponge and custard, having a little nap before casting their votes on important legislation. That place was the real retirement home. Sheldon Oaks was where the action was.

It's a ten-minute walk from Westminster station to Thames House, but it took them twenty-five. Their minds were still quick but their bodies weren't. Carol had butterflies in her tummy. She was about to enter the home of MI5.

'Is there a level above yours?' she asked Margaret.

'If there is I don't know of it.'

'Top secret?'

'The very tippity top. I was home secretary. That counts for something.'

'But that was so long ago.'

'Clearance is clearance. They don't take it back. Not unless you do something very naughty and, unlike you, Carol, I've always been a bit of a goody-goody.'

'Do you still read the reports?'

Margaret laughed. 'No.'

'But there must be so many secrets. Don't you want to know everything?'

'Most of the secrets are very, very boring and the ones that aren't boring, well, I prefer not to know. I like my sleep.'

Carol raised her eyebrows, pondering that there must be a world out there even darker than the one in which she used to operate. And then something occurred to her ... 'Didn't you used to read up on all your colleagues? You said something about the foreign secretary and leather. Aren't there lots of juicy sex scandals and perverts to read about?'

Margaret shook her head wistfully. 'Not these days. I'm afraid the politicians of today are an incredibly boring bunch.'

If the façade of Thames House was neo-classical the lobby was very much not. All glass and security barriers, TVs showing BBC News, police holding semi-automatic weapons, their fingers resting close to the triggers.

'Can I help?'

'Yes, we're looking for some ... What are they called? *Video games*? I'm buying my grandson a present.'

The lady behind the desk gave them both a sickly smile. 'I think you might be lost.'

'This isn't HMV?'

'No, this is ... I think where you need—'

'Just a little joke, dear,' said Margaret. 'It's Margaret. I'm here to see Sir Jeremy. He's expecting me.'

And with that, Sir Jeremy Yallop, the slickly suited head of MI5 appeared behind them. 'Ladies. Follow me.' He swept them through the security barriers.

Carol turned to the girl at the desk and stuck out her tongue for the fun of it. She didn't know what she'd been expecting, but she found the building disappointing. Just normal corridors and normal rooms with normal-looking people in them. Wasn't this the nerve centre of British intelligence? A fortress of state control? There were vending machines with packets of Skips in them. That didn't seem right to her.

Sir Jeremy stopped at a door and opened it. 'All right. Devices.'

'Hand him your phone,' said Margaret, taking hers from her handbag and giving it to Sir Jeremy. Carol did the same.

'I don't usually do plus ones,' said Sir Jeremy, 'but this lady,' he nodded at Margaret, 'saved the country ... What's your estimate, Margaret? Twenty times?'

Margaret blushed. 'Oh, don't be silly. No more than five.'

Carol looked at Margaret in admiration. So many stories, yet she knew she'd never tell.

The room was small. A functional table, like you might find

in any other government building, like something from the office of a school headmaster, with two functional chairs. On the table was a file.

'That's everything we have on Sir Desmond Crisp,' said Sir Jeremy. 'Is there anything else we can get you?'

Carol looked over her shoulder, then lowered her voice. 'Do you have anything on aliens?'

'That'll be all for now, Jeremy,' said Margaret, smiling like a parent covering for her toddler. 'Thank you.'

'Enjoy!'

And with that Sir Jeremy shut the door and left them alone. Carol looked at Margaret and opened her mouth wide in silent excitement. They sat down, eyeing the file as if it was a sacred relic, neither daring to be the first to touch it. Margaret took a bag of sweets from her handbag and offered it to Carol. 'Percy Pig?'

The two ladies quietly worked their way through the file, Carol carefully reading every page and passing it on to Margaret. Every now and then one of the pair would make a noise to indicate that they'd found something interesting. Carol had never been much of a swot but it gave her fond memories of the focus she'd had when writing her diaries, all those years ago.

When they had finished they sat back and looked at each other. Margaret exhaled in shock.

'Well, well, well,' said Carol.

Just then, Sir Jeremy Yallop popped his head around the door with a friendly smile.

'Ah, looks like you're done. I hope you got everything you needed? I can escort you out now if you'd like.'

'Yes, I think that's—' Margaret was gathering her things but Carol interrupted her.

'I'm always reading in the newspapers how you can spy on all of us online.'

Yallop tilted his head to the side, bemused by the tenacious pensioner before him. 'Oh, yes?'

'Well?' said Carol. 'Can you?'

'To a degree.'

'To how much of a degree?'

'Quite a big one.'

'So, if we were to give you a name or two, would you be able to help us look at their communications?'

Sir Jeremy adopted a firmer tone, attempting to draw a line. 'That's really not ... This is all very ... There is the matter of ethics.'

Margaret spoke up. 'You know they're always inviting me to join the Lords Intelligence and Security Committee. I usually say I'm done with all that sort of thing but being in Westminster today makes me wonder if I should get more involved. They have quite a lot of sway when it comes to things like funding, I'm told.'

Yallop yielded. 'I'll get one of our technical people to help you.'

'Thank you.' Margaret gave him a beaming smile like he was a kindly young gentleman who'd offered to help her cross the road.

Just as he was leaving, Carol chipped in: 'Actually,' she said, 'come to think of it, there's one more person's file we'd like a look at. If that's okay?'

Sir Jeremy rolled his eyes, accepting his fate as a man destined to do whatever these two ladies asked of him.

FORTY-TWO

Geoffrey looked down at his pubic hair and considered his own mortality. He'd always shaved his face, had a haircut once a fortnight, but hair from the shoulders down just grew as it grew, like an undisturbed patch of woodland on the edge of town. In old age it had grown into a white, cloud-like mound, like a small sheep. It was just another part of his body, like an elbow. It was what it was. The men of today, they apparently trimmed, shaped, some of them – he'd learnt – even shaved. The idea that there was some kind of cosmetic choice to be made had never occurred to him. Tampering with his pubes crossed some moral line he couldn't articulate. Geoffrey was a strong advocate of the green belt, but maybe this wasn't like the green belt. Maybe pubes were a brownfield site.

He'd never felt so old.

And now Carol and Margaret had gone off on some secret mission and excluded him. He *was* the ex-detective, wasn't he? Shouldn't he be at the centre of things? But they didn't see him like that, did they? No one did. Geoffrey Standing wasn't a copper any more. He was just an old man. There was no place for him, no need for him. Is there anything more redundant than an old man? Old ladies, at least they were still in charge of the grandchildren's birthday cards. Old men? Once they were no longer DIY-fit, what were they for? Geoffrey Standing was irrelevant. He took the nail scissors from his bathroom counter and carefully set about trimming.

Catherine hadn't complained when Carol and Margaret had left but that didn't mean it hadn't hurt. This case was as much hers as it was theirs. What gave them the right to take ownership of it? She and Geoffrey had been instructed to sit tight. *Instructed.*

Were they chasing Shep? Were they in danger? Did Carol and Margaret disapprove of the burgeoning 'romance' – if you could call it that – between her and Geoffrey? Had they been sidelined as punishment?

Catherine placed her book, some vacuous mystery that made little sense to her, on the coffee-table. There was no point in pretending she could read it. Beside the book was the phone, Giles's phone. Really, she should have handed it in when the police took the body but she hadn't been ready to let go. While she had that phone, Catherine was still an investigator, working the case, so she'd pocketed it. Once they'd got into it using his dead face, she'd changed the settings so that it didn't automatically lock. Now she could nose around Giles's phone as much as she liked, as long as she was willing to cross the moral boundary of invading a dead man's privacy.

'Morality', for Catherine, was greyer than ever before. She'd read through the hellish diaries of a serial killer and chosen, after a brief pause, to remain friends with her. Nobody ever really changes: that was the cliché. But here was Catherine, well into her eighth decade, and she *was* changing.

Either she was maturing, growing to appreciate nuance – that there was no good and evil, no black and white, only grey – *or* she was simply becoming a bad person. Whichever it was, she had no time to wallow in self-analysis. Catherine had to see what was in that phone, but first she would need a co-conspirator.

'Catherine, I'm afraid I'm currently not available for sex.' Geoffrey looked at his feet in shame. 'I've injured my penis.'

Catherine closed Geoffrey's front door behind her. She didn't want to ask but had to know. 'How?'

'Not with another woman, you understand,' he said hastily. 'I had an accident with some nail scissors. I think it should be out of action for at least a fortnight but I'd be very happy to provide you with oral pleasure if you think that will tide you over.'

Catherine slammed down her handbag on Geoffrey's kitchen table, hoping the shock would move the conversation on. 'I think we should explore Giles's phone,' she said.

There was no moral struggle for Geoffrey and they immediately set about trawling through the dead man's life. At first, they found little – hardly any text messages, plenty of unanswered emails from his accountant. A health app stored tracks of each of his daily runs; the notes app contained terrible moneymaking ideas – 'Write a novel?' It was Catherine who saw the WhatsApp logo. Geoffrey hadn't heard of it, so Catherine explained it was an encrypted messaging service. Her family had insisted she joined a group on the app so that they could arrange Christmas.

Quite why their Christmas plans had to be encrypted she was never sure, but all her children now messaged her on WhatsApp rather than via text message. Sure enough, this turned out to be where all the action was on Giles's phone.

His most frequent interlocutor by far? Shep Newsom.

They scrolled up, as far back as they could go in the conversation, and read it chronologically, in search of as full a picture as possible. The first thing to become clear was that Giles and Shep had indeed gone to Eton together and shared the same dorm. Beyond the 'bantz', the gifs and the tasteless jokes about old school friends, Catherine and Geoffrey were able gradually to piece together some kind of story. The young men were both obsessed with becoming great business titans, egging each other on, like a shit Gates and Jobs, into bigger and bigger failures. Giles, they discovered, had invested in a number of Shep's doomed schemes: *No problem bud. I got u.* Then, suddenly, about a year ago, Giles had started to ask about returns. *Got a bit of a cash flow probleramo here buddy. How are the old balance sheeteroos looking? Hate to ask but I could do with some profiteroles.* Shep had obfuscated. In the unlikely event that there were any profit-eroles, he didn't appear especially keen to share them.

Then, very recently, just a few days ago, Giles had sent a picture with a caption – *Got a new little businesserami if you want a piece of the action jackson bud?* The picture was of a greenhouse filled with plants. Geoffrey recognised them immediately. 'That's cannabis.'

Catherine took the phone from him. He was right. She thought of a university boyfriend and the cannabis plants he grew on the windowsill in his filthy bedroom. What had become of him? she wondered. Just another old person now, like they all were, she supposed. She inspected the picture closely and spotted that behind the greenhouse was a blue sky and the tops of some trees. The greenhouse wasn't on the ground.

'That's on the roof,' she said, pointing upwards. '*Our* roof.'

Geoffrey looked at the ceiling.

Catherine kept reading the messages between Giles and Shep. 'Oh, wow,' she said. 'Look at this.'

She handed him the phone.

'Well, now, that *is* interesting,' said Geoffrey.

'Let's call the others and tell them,' said Catherine.

Geoffrey slapped his thighs and stood up. 'I'm sure they'll be back soon. We can tell them then.'

'Where are you going?' said Catherine.

'Don't you think we ought to take a look on that bloody roof?'

FORTY-THREE

Carol and Margaret raced back to Sheldon Oaks in a black cab, decadence to Carol's mind but necessary.

Carol knew who the killer was. She knew the whole truth. She knew who had done it, how they had done it and why. She subtly put two fingers to her wrist and felt her pulse. Slow and steady. The tension was rising but Carol remained calm. Good. She'd need poise, considering what was to come.

'Tell me. Please,' Margaret pleaded.

'I may only get to do this once,' said Carol, watching her changed city roll by from the back of the taxi. 'I have to do it right.'

'I really do think dénouements are just a fictional device,' said Margaret. 'I've been involved, in one way or another, in a lot of murder cases and I'm not sure I've ever come across a dénouement in real life. Gathering everyone together and telling the full story. It's just an Agatha Christie thing, Carol. There's really no need.'

Carol looked her friend in the eye. 'Give. Me. My. Dénouement.' She looked to the skies. The clouds suggested rain was on its way.

'Karaoke night tonight,' said Margaret, breaking the brief silence.

Carol, deep in thought, could only respond with 'Mmm'.

A ping on both their phones. Margaret got to hers first. 'It's Catherine. Oh, Christ.'

'What?' said Carol.

'Catherine and Geoffrey have decided to go on the roof.'

Carol leant towards the driver. 'I need you to go a lot faster.'

'I can only go as fast as I can, love.'

'I know. It's just it's very urgent.' Carol turned to Margaret. 'My friend here. She's, uh, in labour.'

The driver assessed them in the rearview mirror and frowned.

'She's had a hard life,' said Carol.

The driver shrugged and set about overtaking a bus.

'I have a question,' said Margaret.

'I'm not telling you who the murderer is,' said Carol.

'No, not that. The roof. It's locked. How are they getting up there?'

FORTY-FOUR

Catherine stuck her hand up her blouse and fumbled around. The corridor was quiet.

'Geoffrey, can you give me a hand with my bra?'

'Catherine, I've ... My penis. It's really quite—'

'Not that!' she said. 'Carol did something with hers. I need the wire.'

Catherine and Geoffrey were at the top of the small flight of stairs that led to the roof door. Catherine undid her two top buttons and Geoffrey, gentleman that he was, did his best to tamper with the bra without engaging with her breasts. Despite their afternoon of carnality, there was still a degree of awkwardness around each other's bodies.

'The fabric. It's too tough. I can't get the wire out.'

'Use your teeth.'

'Catherine. I ... I've only ever been with my wife. Until the other ... You're obviously a lot more experienced. I'm really not accustomed to this kind of ...'

Catherine smiled. She'd managed to get Geoffrey to admit to the one thing he wasn't an expert in. She touched his shoulder.

'I just want the wire. I've an idea. Why don't you just take them out?'

He frowned. 'Take what out?'

'Your teeth,' said Catherine.

And so he did. Geoffrey took out his dentures and clamped them onto Catherine's bra. A couple of tugs and they were able to tear the cotton enough to get at the wire. Catherine fed it through. Realising she'd emasculated Geoffrey, she offered him the chance to unlock the door with the wire, which he proudly did without much trouble.

'Impressive,' said Catherine.

'Let's just say I still know a thing or two about crime.'

'Very good. Don't forget to pop your teeth back in.'

The door opened outwards, revealing the fading light from the grey London sky and leading them directly onto the roof. The surface below their feet was black asphalt, with small puddles dotted around, still there from a morning shower. A brick wall, no more than a couple of feet high, bordered the whole roof. At the rear, to their left, was a large greenhouse, about twenty feet in length. Catherine headed right and leant over the wall. Below her she could see the four brand-new paving stones, still clean.

'This is where Desmond fell,' she said.

'Where he was pushed,' Geoffrey corrected her. 'He'd have to have been playing silly buggers to fall off here.'

For a moment they were quiet, contemplating the death of their friend. Catherine inspected the ground, the wall, the surface of the roof. What was she expecting to find up there? A signed confession from the killer? It was just a roof.

She looked at the greenhouse. It was dense with green plants, nothing else. Marijuana presumably. But they knew that already, didn't they? What did it *tell* them?

Together, they paced towards it.

'That looks like rather a lot of marijuana, doesn't it, Geoffrey?'

'I've never seen so much in one place. That must be worth . . . I'm just trying to think . . .'

'More than a hundred thousand?' asked Catherine.

'Easily.'

Something moved in the greenery.

'Wait,' Catherine whispered, stopping Geoffrey with her hand.

The back of a man's head. Someone was watering the plants. The voice inside hummed an old standard.

'He's wearing earphones,' said Catherine.

Geoffrey edged forwards to get a closer look but stepped into a puddle. His slip-on loafer was no good and his foot was immediately drenched. Instinctively he shouted out: 'Jesus bloody Jesus sodding bloody Christ!'

Catherine held his arm as the head in the greenhouse turned to face them.

Jim.

They stayed still, frozen, as Jim placed down the watering can and went for the greenhouse door. In what felt like a second, he was headed straight towards Geoffrey. No smile, no greeting. He was leaning forward, determined. This was not Jim the friendly old crooner Catherine knew from the karaoke nights. This was Jim the old villain she'd heard about. His footsteps grew louder and quicker.

Jim punched Geoffrey in the face. It was the jab of a man who'd hit people before.

'No!' screamed Catherine.

Geoffrey bent, holding his face. Jim stood over him. 'I'm not letting you fuck me over again, Geoff.'

'I had to do it,' said Geoffrey.

Still bent over, Geoffrey rugby-tackled Jim, pushing him back towards the greenhouse. They moved slowly. Here were two men who still knew how to fight, but at a much gentler pace. Eventually, Jim's back hit the greenhouse. Geoffrey pulled back his fist and lunged but Jim moved to the side, leaving Geoffrey to punch the glass, breaking it and cutting his hand. With the panel broken, Geoffrey improvised, putting his arm inside the greenhouse, picking up a pair of secateurs and turning to face Jim.

'What are you gonna do, Geoff?' shouted Jim. 'Prune me?'

Slowly pacing backwards, Jim picked up a waist-high spade that was propped against the greenhouse. The two old men were in a stand-off, each holding up their horticultural weapon of choice towards the other.

Carol and Margaret arrived at the entrance to the roof sweaty with adrenaline. The door was ajar and the police cordon had been pulled aside. They looked at each other.

'Ready?' said Carol.

'Wait,' said Margaret, taking a makeup mirror out of her handbag and wiping ketchup that had been there for God knew how long from the side of her mouth.

'What are you doing?' said Carol.

'If I'm about to die, I want to look my best.'

'You look lovely.'

They opened the door and found the action already in progress. Carol and Margaret headed for Catherine and planted themselves beside her, watching the two men the whole time. Margaret offered Catherine a Percy Pig, which she silently refused.

'What's going on?' said Margaret.

'We found Jim in the greenhouse watering some cannabis plants. When we saw each other, he punched Geoffrey. Now they're in some kind of stand-off,' Catherine whispered. 'It feels like an old fight, like they have history.'

'They do,' said Carol, biting the ear off a Percy Pig.

'You ruined my life,' said Jim.

'You ruined your own life,' said Geoffrey.

'You could of helped me. I asked you for help, Geoff,' said Jim.

'Could *have*,' said Geoffrey. '*Could have* helped me. You see, people shorten "could have" to "could've" and then they think that "'ve" is "of" but it is actually, as I say, "could *have*".'

'Jesus Christ, you're such an arsehole,' said Jim.

'Right,' said Catherine. 'I'm completely lost. What are they talking about?'

'Grammar, I think,' said Carol.

'No, before that,' said Catherine.

The three women were standing in a row, watching the action. From behind, you might think they were waiting for a bus.

'Right. So. Jim was a police officer,' said Carol. Jim turned towards her. 'Stop me if I go wrong at any point, boys. Jim was a police officer and he went undercover with the McConvilles, who were big around here back in the day.'

Catherine was conscious that Geoffrey was taking small, nervous steps forwards, slowly moving the stand-off towards the roof's edge.

'I'm listening,' said Margaret, putting more sweets into her mouth.

'How did you find all this out?' asked Catherine.

'Margaret took me on a little trip to MI5. We had a look at Jim's file,' said Carol.

Catherine was impressed. 'Wow.'

'Oh, you wouldn't believe it, Catherine,' said Carol. 'They've got files on everyone. You should see the size of yours.'

Catherine turned to her in shock.

'Just a little joke,' said Carol.

Catherine hit Carol on the arm then returned to the topic of the moment. 'Okay, so Jim was undercover?'

'Yes,' said Carol. 'But I'm guessing he was too good at it. Would that be fair to say, Jim?'

'You could say that, yeah.'

'Jim made a good fake criminal,' said Carol. 'So good, in fact, that he made a very good *real* criminal. Did a murder or two.'

'Or three!' said Geoffrey, spitting from his bloodied mouth, but still holding up the secateurs. His eyes never left Jim. Catherine, to her surprise, had never found him more attractive.

'Now, once you're in so deep that you start killing people for a crime gang,' said Carol, 'are you even a police officer any more? How can they let you back in? But, Jim, I'm guessing you still thought you were a copper. You weren't supposed to turn into an actual villain, you just did. I know how you feel.'

'We're not the same!' shouted Jim. 'I killed because I was ordered to.'

'Oh, don't be so pedantic!' snapped Carol.

'Wait, wait, wait,' said Catherine. 'Finish the story.'

'Pretty simple, I think,' said Carol. 'Jim wanted his old life as a police officer back. I'm guessing you, Geoffrey, were one of the people who wouldn't let him back in. So Jim stayed in the Mafia, got himself all the way to the top.'

Margaret finished the last of the Percy Pigs and put the packet into her handbag. 'Was absolutely *everybody* in Sheldon Oaks an investigator at some point?'

'I wasn't,' said Carol. 'But I am now.'

'Hang on,' said Catherine.

The men were still circling each other with their weapons up, neither taking his eyes off the other. Something had to break.

Catherine continued, 'Why didn't the police just arrest Jim? If he was a criminal now, that is. Why would they just leave him to be a gangster?'

'Because of Desmond!' shouted Geoffrey.

'Desmond,' said Carol.

'Because Desmond was bent,' said Margaret, clocking on.

'In Jim, Desmond had a man at the centre of a crime gang,' said Carol. 'And in Desmond, Jim had the man at the top of the Met. Together, they ran North London. Two cheeks of the same arse.'

Carol felt a drop of rain. It was spitting, the kind of rain you get just before a heavy shower. Then Geoffrey made the error that would change all their lives for ever. He looked up at the sky. Jim took the opportunity to whack the secateurs out of his hand with the spade. Geoffrey was weaponless, but his body, under threat, remembered a move from fifty years ago, and did what must have been the slowest roundhouse kick in history.

'Ow! My hip! My bloody hip!' shouted Geoffrey.

But the kick had done its job and the spade went flying over the wall. After a second, they heard a clang as it hit the ground below. Geoffrey powered forward, applying his weight advantage, pushing Jim against the wall. But Jim was tough. Muscle memory took over. He'd been there before, fighting for his life. He was, quite simply, the stronger man. The men grappled, Jim's head hanging backwards over the wall.

Jim turned his head, glancing at the ground many feet below. The view served as a defibrillator and he found another gear, forcing Geoffrey back and spinning him around. Now Jim was on top with Geoffrey hanging over the wall. Just one final push and Geoffrey would fall to his death. Jim's body had no doubt, no hesitation. He wanted Geoffrey dead and Carol could see it.

Carol was in the moment.

Carol was present.

Carol could not let her friend die.

She ran, surprising herself at how fast her aged body could go, and grabbed Geoffrey's flailing arm. She tugged him, by the wrist, out of Jim's hold. The unexpected nature of her move caused Jim to slip, smacking his chin against the edge of the small wall and landing face down on the asphalt. Carol sank her knee into the back of his neck.

She heard a whimper, not from Jim but from Geoffrey, who was now sitting on the floor quivering, contemplating how close he'd come to death.

What now? It was four against one and Jim had no weapon. Carol was in the zone. She could ease the life out of him right here, snap his neck, strangle him. It would be nice to feel the old buzz. The moment when you take a man from one realm to another, when *you* flick the switch. The privilege.

Time slowed.

Just as she was about to begin the kill, something new arrived: hesitation. She looked up at Geoffrey, Catherine and Margaret. Her friends. These people didn't have that impulse. For perhaps the first time in her life, Carol had something to lose.

She didn't *need* to kill Jim. They had the upper hand. He wasn't a threat any more. The exertions of the last few minutes had taken their toll on him. This was a man whose body couldn't do what his mind wanted any more and Carol's mind didn't want to do what her body could. To kill him now would be to do it for sport. No need to kill for killing's sake.

As Carol took away her knee she heard the footsteps coming ...

And then watched the secateurs go into the back of Jim's neck. Hard and deep. It happened in slow motion. Was this an out-of-body experience? Had her muscle memory taken over? It took her a full second to comprehend the new reality.

'*Don't hurt my man!*' Catherine shouted.

Carol moved to the side and saw Catherine's contorted face, red with rage, her teeth gritted, as she stabbed Jim three times.

Is that what I used to look like? Carol pondered.

Carol, Margaret, Geoffrey and Catherine sat on the roof, their backs leaning against the small wall. They were all breathless, so overwhelmed by the action that they hardly noticed the rain. Catherine looked at the blood on her hand and dropped the secateurs. Jim lay dead, his face resting in a puddle.

Margaret broke the silence. 'At least we know who killed Desmond and Giles now.'

'It wasn't Jim,' said Carol, matter-of-factly.

'It *wasn't*?' said Margaret.

'Nope.'

'The drugs ... Sorry, Jim was watering them. Am I being thick?' said Catherine. 'I'm really not sure what's going on.'

'All will be revealed,' said Carol.

'When?' said Geoffrey. 'I was hoping to watch *Grand Designs* at nine.'

'At the dénouement, of course,' said Carol.

'And when is that exactly?' said Margaret. 'Did you send an invitation? Sorry, I haven't had a chance to check my phone.'

'Now. Downstairs, in the hall.' She looked at Jim's corpse. 'Unfortunately, not everyone can make it but I'm expecting a good turnout. It's karaoke night! You can't miss karaoke night!'

'And Jim's body?' said Geoffrey.

Carol thought for a moment, looking at Catherine.

'Leave him here,' she said. 'We can deal with all that later.'

'There's only one problem,' said Margaret. They looked at her. 'I'm really not sure I can get up.'

FORTY-FIVE

Everyone was there. Those who were still alive, anyway. The death toll stood at three. For one brief week in July, London's murder hot spot was a luxury retirement home in Hampstead.

Karaoke night.

Carol took a deep breath, centring herself. Beside her, sitting at a round table, close to the stage area in the home's ballroom, were Catherine, Geoffrey and Margaret. Her friends. The first people she could ever really, truly call her friends for the simple reason that they had accepted her for who she was. Not an easy thing to do in her case. They had seen her very depths and stood by her.

Catherine and Geoffrey held hands, both had puffy eyes from crying, the events of less than an hour ago still with them. Geoffrey's other hand was wrapped in a bandage. Margaret was wired, cleaning her teeth with her tongue, waiting for Carol's big moment.

Carol checked again that everybody was in the room. She'd contacted all of the concerned parties and promised the truth. *Karaoke night: be there.* If she was going to do a dénouement, she was going to do it right. Time to deliver.

Belinda was on the microphone admirably trying and failing to hit each and every note of 'I Will Always Love You'. Her new boyfriend, Marco, looked on from the bar, straining every sinew to give an authentically supportive smile. Tyler was on the decks, going through the scraps of paper that bore requests to sing. Elisa scuttled around the room, pointing at bar staff to do this or that, apparently overwhelmed by the unusually large turnout, no doubt surprised to see so many non-residents. DS Laura Welsh and DCI Bob Beattie were at a table on the opposite side of the dance-floor, Laura nervously watching Carol's every move, Bob rolling a cigarette. Even Dr Stephen Turnham, the pathologist, and his bubbly assistant, Gemma, had joined them at the table, not wanting to miss the show. They looked pleased to be on a rare night out. At another table Helen and Shep Newsom, empty cocktail glasses in front of them, stared vacantly into space. Polly's face flickered in the disco lights, her attention on her knitting, her pupils dilated from being reunited with her hash stash.

Every face in the room grimaced as Belinda went all out for that big, long Whitney Houston note. Tyler took that as his cue to fade her out.

'Let's hear it for Belinda. So many songs to get through tonight. So many songs.'

Tyler spoke in a kind of imitation DJ voice, reminding Carol of Simon Bates, on that day in the van, all those years ago. The applause was polite but not enthusiastic.

'All right, next up we have Carol Quinn. Carol Quinn to the stage, please. Carol Quinn.'

Carol took another deep breath. Margaret stood up and

whispered in her ear, 'I have a knife in my handbag. If you need me to use it, just give me the nod.'

'Thank you, Margaret,' said Carol. Everyone had changed that week, in one way or another.

Carol felt the eyes of the room on her as she walked to the microphone. The eyes of Sheldon Oaks had been on her ever since Desmond's murder.

'Carol's gonna be singing "My Heart Will Go On". Let's give her some support, round of applause for Carol!'

Tyler handed the karaoke mic to Carol. She tentatively took hold of it. She'd never held a microphone before, but tonight she felt ready to take centre-stage.

'Actually, everybody,' Carol began, 'I have something to say. I'd like to speak with you all for a moment about what's been on all our minds for the last few days. A couple of weeks ago, you all learnt about my past as a serial killer. Then, over the course of the last two weeks, people have been murdered. I'm here to tell you that those murders and my presence here *are not connected*. Ladies and gentlemen, I know who murdered Sir Desmond Crisp and I know who murdered Giles Temple. If you'll give me a moment, I'll tell you.'

The panpipes from the karaoke backing track to 'My Heart Will Go On' were still playing, giving Carol's speech a sentimental undertone.

'Actually, Tyler, would you mind turning the music down? Thank you.' Carol had the room's attention in a way that no Vera Lynn tribute act ever could. Nothing drags people in like a promise to tell the truth.

'When Desmond died, I knew eyes would fall on me, and so

they did. I was starting to love it here at Sheldon Oaks. I was, for the first time in my life, making ...' Carol looked to her group and surprised herself with the emotion in her voice '... friends. I realised that the only way I could stay here was by clearing my name.'

Carol's only ever experience in public speaking had been sixty years ago, when she'd been asked to make a contribution to the South London Schools Debating Competition and presented a case for women in the workplace. She approached her dénouement with a similarly methodical outlining of the facts.

'Ladies and gentlemen, Sir Desmond Crisp was killed by poisoning, bludgeoning, strangulation, and by being pushed off the roof of this building. Let's deal with each of those in turn.'

Carol noticed Margaret get more comfortable in her seat, as if she was watching the opening credits to a good film.

'Poisoning,' said Carol, holding up a thumb, denoting the number one. 'Desmond was poisoned but what with and by whom? The autopsy revealed that Desmond's last meal was shepherd's pie, a dish that just so happened to be on the lunch menu in the Apple Tree on the day of his death. That led us to consider Marco, a man who could easily have tampered with Desmond's meal, and incidentally, the new boyfriend of one of our favourite residents, Belinda LaBelle.'

'These accusations must stop!' yelled Belinda with heightened, soap opera-style emotion.

'And they will,' said Carol, 'if you'll let me explain. You see, I found Belinda's outburst on the evening the police came to talk with us rather over the top. I thought she must be hiding something, that perhaps she and her man had tricked Desmond into giving her his fortune before knocking him off. The truth is, Belinda is just a highly emotional, highly sexed individual. So highly sexed, in fact, that their alibi is the love that they were making in the snooker room at the exact time of Desmond's murder. As I discovered yesterday, the snooker room is just one of many places in this building Belinda and Marco like to ... *express* their love for each other. They book it out but never think to go to Reception and collect a set of balls. I guess you bring your own, Marco? I've checked back through the bookings, and at the time of Desmond's murder, Belinda and Marco had reserved the snooker room. I wish the pair of you a very happy life together. Oh, I nearly forgot ...'

Carol took something from her pocket and threw it at Belinda. 'I found your knickers in the green pocket.'

Belinda caught them and put them into her handbag, blushing. Warming to her Poirot moment, Carol moved on to the next piece of the puzzle. 'Dr Turnham?'

The enthralled pathologist looked surprised to be called upon. 'Yes?'

'What meat is in shepherd's pie?'

'Uh ... beef.'

Geoffrey gasped and the whole room heard it.

'Geoffrey,' said Carol, 'would you like to inform the room what meat is in a shepherd's pie? You're a stickler for this sort of thing, aren't you? I'm confident you know.'

Geoffrey stood up and delivered his answer solemnly. 'Lamb. The answer is lamb.'

'That's right, Geoffrey,' said Carol. 'While we're on the

subject, is there a similar pie that *does* contain beef? If so, what is it called?'

'Cottage pie,' said Geoffrey, almost adding 'your honour,' then sitting down.

'Cottage. Pie,' said Carol. 'Don't feel bad about it, Dr Turnham, it's a very common error but it is an error that sent us down the wrong path. I'm sure Geoffrey would have spotted it himself in the autopsy, but I'm told he was feeling a little queasy. Desmond didn't have shepherd's pie that day. He had cottage pie and he had it somewhere else. But we'll get to that.'

Carol looked at her table of allies. Margaret, Catherine and Geoffrey's mouths were agape in admiration. It gave her the confidence to continue. She held up her thumb and forefinger. 'Bludgeoning. Desmond was hit on the head by a blunt object that had a flat circular surface, with a diameter of roughly forty-five centimetres. My first thought was a croquet mallet. They are readily available at Sheldon Oaks. Jim, who unfortunately can't be with us this evening, was a regular on the croquet lawn and had experience with murder. But there are two problems with that: our murderer was left-handed, while Jim was not. And our croquet mallets do not match the indentation on Desmond's head. I know because I measured one this morning. There is one mallet missing from Sheldon Oaks, though. The gardening mallet. If anyone is interested, by the way, the top-selling gardening mallet on Amazon just so happens to have a surface diameter of forty-five centimetres.

'While we're on the subject of gardening tools, let's come to strangling. The autopsy suggested that whoever strangled

Desmond didn't do it with their bare hands. I wonder if they could have been wearing gardening gloves. Tyler?'

Tyler, headphones still around his neck, was in denial. 'You don't know nothing!'

'Geoffrey, you're our resident grammar expert. What was that?' asked Carol.

'A double negative,' said Geoffrey.

'That's right. A double negative. You're right, Tyler. I don't know nothing. In fact, I know rather a lot. I know that you took Desmond up onto the roof. You had a key. I know that the cleaner stopped vacuuming because she saw you do it. Is that why she had to be sacked? What did you do, Elisa? Send her off to Thailand for a few months as a redundancy package? And, Tyler, I also know that you bludgeoned him on the head with the gardening mallet – with your left hand. See, I thought you were right-handed, but then Catherine said something about her grandson. *Plays cricket with his right hand, tennis with his left.* Some people are like that, aren't they? Ambidextrous? You're very comfortable on those decks. I guess you fix fences with your right hand and murder with your left. What happened to the rope fence by the way? You never finished the job. Did you lose your mallet? Or did you decide you had to throw it away?

'And then, finally, you pushed him. That's a very distinctive jumper you're wearing, Tyler. The fabric you left on Desmond led us to Polly. But Polly didn't murder Desmond. Polly is in a world of her own and that's all thanks to you, Tyler, because you've been providing her with hash cakes. Which is why she knitted you the jumper. As a thank-you.' Carol smiled. 'I love it when the different generations get along.'

Tyler's eyes were darting around the room.

'You could try and make a run for it but I don't think you'd get very far. The police are sitting right over there. Why don't you just sit still for a moment and I'll tell everyone why you did it? I've got something that may help to reduce your sentence. You didn't do it on your own. You were only helping your mother. Wasn't he, Elisa?'

Elisa stood frozen, by the bar.

'Ferragudo. That's where our friend Elisa is from. I've never been but it's beautiful, isn't it, Polly?'

Polly slowly nodded.

'I know Elisa doesn't look it but, would you believe she turns fifty next year? Funnily enough, fifty years ago was when Polly and Desmond went to Ferragudo on their honeymoon. Desmond got a waitress pregnant. That waitress was Elisa's mother. When you showed me the picture, I wondered why anyone would want to leave such a place. You were looking for your father. I wondered where a lady of your complexion might have got those bright blue eyes. I don't know how long it took for him to show an interest, but you were so determined that when he retired you came to work here. Got your son a job here too. Elisa, you got to know your dad at Sheldon Oaks and Desmond was a gentler man in his later years. He didn't shun you, I imagine, but did he show you love?'

Elisa took her glasses off and wiped her eyes.

'Not enough, I'm sure, to make up for all the lost time. Certainly not enough to put you in his will. Think of the life you and Tyler could have had if he'd supported you the way he did these embarrassments.' Carol gestured towards the

Newsoms. 'I empathise, Elisa, I really do. He made you both angry and that is reason enough to kill someone. Certainly was for me. Of course, you were the one who told me Polly had been married to Desmond. You were looking to give me a suspect to throw me off the scent but all you did was lead me to your door. Did you hold a grudge against Polly? That doesn't seem fair. All she did was marry the wrong man.'

Polly now had a thousand-mile stare, lost in the past.

'I was up all night on Facebook,' said Carol. 'You young folks, you don't bother with Facebook any more, do you? It's all Instagram – and what's that other one, Tyler? TokTok? TikTok? But plenty of us old folks love Facebook. Some of us put everything on there! I suppose it's a way of feeling like we're still in touch with the world and you told us all to learn how to use it fifteen years ago and now that we've figured it out you're telling us we need to go on some other app. It's ridiculous!'

There was a murmur of approval from the residents at Carol's brief rant.

'Desmond had a Facebook account, you see. You probably didn't even know. He wrote a status on the day he died. Do you know what it said?'

Elisa shook her head.

Looking forward to cottage pie with my daughter today. Yum yum! Little did he know that you would pack his cottage pie with deadly nightshade. I went for a walk in the gardens this morning and checked the flowerbeds. Among the deadly nightshade, there's a clump missing. It's been pulled right off the stalks. You knew it could kill, didn't you, Elisa? That's what a quick Google search will tell you.'

Elisa held on to the edge of the bar, her other hand shaking.

'Who killed Giles?' shouted Agatha. 'And what colour were they?'

'Yes! Giles!' said Carol, clapping her hands together. 'Funny you should ask that, Agatha. I'll rattle through this one as quick as I can. I know you were all looking forward to the karaoke. I don't think I'll surprise any of you if I say that Giles Temple was a suspect. I've had a look through his accounts and the man was in trouble. The fact is, money is a good enough reason for anyone to kill, but why Desmond Crisp? If Giles had a motive, I never found it, and when he himself was murdered, I knew he wasn't responsible.

'Elisa couldn't stand to see an idiot like Giles Temple be given so many breaks in life, only to cock them all up. It was people like her who deserved a chance. She knew that Giles wasn't on top of his finances, never understood his statements, never spoke to his accountant. His money seemed to keep disappearing. He couldn't understand it. You were stealing it, weren't you, Elisa? The Sheldon Oaks accounts at Companies House look awfully peculiar. You've got a little account somewhere, haven't you? An awful lot of money from Sheldon Oaks Ltd seems to be going to a business in Portugal. You also managed to change his will. That office of his is such a mess. Documents everywhere. I managed to take a peep at a few when you nipped out for a conversation with your son. What were you talking about? Murder? You knew Giles never looked at the documents you gave him to sign. But then, on the day he was murdered, he texted you to say he was about to sell this place to someone who had just come into some money: Shep Newsom.'

Helen Newsom dropped a glass in cartoon fashion.

'Oh dear,' said Carol. 'Maybe Shep was going to tell you for your birthday, Helen. "I've bought you an old folks' home, darling." Elisa, you couldn't let that happen, could you? You'd worked so hard to get everything in place. When the police lost interest you'd find a way to knock off Giles and this place would be yours. But him saying he'd sell it to Shep, well, that was a spanner in the works. The timing was far from ideal, Polly was at the police station, but you had to kill him before he sold it off. You knew he'd burn through the money he got for it in weeks and then there'd be nothing for you in the will.'

Elisa tried to scream but her vocal cords were tight and it came out like a whimper. 'I didn't kill Giles!'

'No, you didn't. Maybe it was just a case of someone beating you to it or maybe two murders was one too many for you. Lightweight.'

Margaret laughed at her serial-killer friend's joke.

'Elisa didn't kill Giles Temple,' said Carol. 'Detective Chief Inspector Bob Beattie did.'

Audible gasps hit Carol in stereo. Bob felt Laura's gaze on him and looked away.

'Giles Temple only ever had one successful business: growing marijuana on the Sheldon Oaks roof. Rather a lot of it in fact. Much of it ended up in cakes. Good to know that the baking group and I weren't the only ones using the communal kitchen. Running an operation that big in the middle of London required help, and Giles had rather a lot. Giles was a pampered posh boy. He didn't have connections in the underworld. How would he sell all that dope? Jim . . . Jim still had a foot in a local operation and was able to help Giles get his crop out to the market. Some of my old prison friends were able to confirm that one for me.

'Jim gave him a connection in the underworld, but in order for Giles's little business to work he needed one in the – I don't know, what would you call the police? The overworld? You can't grow that much weed on a Hampstead roof without paying off the cops. Right, Detective Chief Inspector Beattie? The only way you could afford to put your mum in here is because it didn't cost you a penny. There's a reason why the roof was cordoned off, why you never let Laura up there, and it was nothing to do with how Desmond died. You just didn't want Laura to know about your dodgy side hustle. I hope you at least get the rounds in at the pub, Bob.'

Laura's jaw dropped.

'But Giles had real money problems and they were driving him crazy, making him do silly things. Like blackmailing you. Did he threaten to tell Internal Investigations that you were just another dodgy cop? Whatever he said, you knew you had to get rid of him. You know what they do to cops in prison. Things had got out of hand. Giles was too chaotic, couldn't be trusted. So you did it then. You burnt him alive. I had Catherine check for me and you signed the Sheldon Oaks visitors' book just before Giles was locked in the sauna. I'm sure, being a man on the inside, you had your own key.'

Bob, now chewing on nicotine gum, was fighting for his life. 'I was visiting my mum! You can't prove nothing! I was visiting my mum!'

Carol spoke softly: 'But, Detective Chief Inspector Beattie, your mother wasn't here. She was on the trip to see *Mamma Mia*. I watched her getting into the minibus.'

Bob Beattie slumped, crumbling into himself, another man beaten by Carol Quinn.

'I hope you enjoyed the show, Agatha. What's your favourite Abba song? I always liked "Does Your Mother Know". I feel for you, Bob, I really do. I've always tried not to get involved in other people's murders but the only way I could keep my friends was by clearing my name. You see . . .' Carol looked at Margaret, Catherine and Geoffrey, who all smiled at her in admiration '. . . my friends mean a lot to me.'

The room sat in stunned silence. So much information, all of it shocking.

'That's how you do a dénouement,' said Margaret.

'Let's have some music, shall we?' said Carol, leaning over Tyler's desk and pushing up the volume, karaoke panpipes from the opening bars of 'My Heart Will Go On' filling the room. Laura stared daggers at Bob Beattie. Elisa stepped behind the bar and poured herself a large whisky. Tyler continued to sob. With no one knowing quite what to do, Carol chose to sing the song.

FORTY-SIX

The guard hit the switch and the fluorescent lights flickered on. If there was one criticism to be levelled at prison visiting rooms, it was the lighting. Too bright. Yes, yes, this is a correctional facility but there is such a thing as cruel and unusual punishment. Come on, she thought. No one looks their best here. Dim the lights.

The twenty or so inmates each shuffled to a table. They were all so young. It happens so quickly. One minute you're the new kid, next you're the little old lady in the corner, the one who's seen it all before.

The guard on the other side of the room opened the door and the visitors made their way in. Some nervous, taking it all in, tears already flowing. *How had it come to this?* Some on their thousandth visit. Just another errand, another day in the month, the one where you visit Stephanie, your daughter, the one who shot the postman.

Carol heard her visitors before she saw them. Geoffrey was admonishing a guard for the lax security. 'I could be smuggling any number of things in my downstairs cavity but you wouldn't know, would you? Why? Because you didn't check.'

Carol gave them all a smile as they arrived at her table. A guard helpfully found an extra chair so there were enough for three.

They were silent for a moment, contemplating the events that had led them to this.

'How are you?' said Margaret.

'I'm good,' said Carol, lightly. 'The menu's changed. Used to be pasta on a Thursday. Now it's chicken curry.'

'Oh dear,' said Margaret. 'Any good?'

'Oh no, it's an improvement. Can't complain.'

'Well, that's nice.'

Margaret filled Carol in on all the gossip. Belinda and Marco were no longer a thing, Belinda having decided that she wasn't ready to settle down. Polly had gone cold turkey, made a return to writing and had a new book coming out later in the year. A murder mystery set in a retirement home. There was a market for that sort of thing now, apparently. DCI Bob Beattie had been arrested for corruption and had 'given up smoking'. Detective Sergeant Laura Welsh was now Detective Inspector Welsh and hoping to find time for a beach holiday. Margaret had heard she was dating a man and said it would be nice if they got married so her accent didn't clash with her surname any more. Catherine said not everyone took their husband's surname now. Margaret said she'd be silly not to, 'Unless his name is English!' and they all laughed.

Shep and Helen Newsom had bought Sheldon Oaks and were running the place. Shep's expensive lawyers had managed to help him get away with a suspended sentence on the grounds that he was too dim to realise he'd invested in a drugs business.

Nothing much had changed in the home, really. Karaoke night was still a thing, and with Jim no longer the star, Geoffrey had plucked up the courage to sing, specialising in national anthems, to give the evening an educational element. There had been the odd death, as always, but they tended to be a lot less dramatic these days. Agatha had fallen to lung cancer.

'Apparently her lungs were black,' said Margaret.

'Well, she wouldn't have liked that,' said Carol.

Tyler was in some prison up north, awaiting trial. Wakefield, Margaret had heard.

'Do you see Elisa at all?' asked Margaret.

'Oh, yes, didn't I tell you? We're sharing a cell,' said Carol. 'She told me to say hello, by the way. Didn't want to come out today. I think she's a bit embarrassed. I keep telling her, just because you're a killer, it doesn't make you a bad person. She'll be okay. I've been showing her the ropes.'

Geoffrey was jumpy, feeling he should be doing something, helping out the guards somehow. Catherine was quiet.

'Oh! Oh!' Margaret was getting excited. 'Show Carol the ring!'

Catherine, blushing, put her hand on the table.

Carol's eyes widened. 'Is this . . .?'

'Yes,' said Catherine. 'We're getting married in the spring.'

'Geoffrey!' said Carol.

'Well, you know, she's up the duff so I thought I better do the decent thing!' He said it loudly so the whole room could hear, letting out a massive laugh.

Catherine hit him.

'We're all getting a bit bored with that joke,' said Margaret.

Catherine took a deep breath and looked Carol in the eyes. 'Thank you. I'm so ...' her voice quivered as she said it '... grateful.'

'I know,' said Carol.

'No, Carol, I don't think you do.'

'Catherine, it's okay. You belong out there and I belong in here. Everything in its right place.'

'I don't accept that,' said Catherine. 'I'm so sorry.'

'It is what it is,' said Carol.

'But ...' Catherine whispered, tears on her cheeks. 'You didn't kill Jim. I did.'

'Friends help friends, don't they?'

'I've already set things in motion to appeal the sentence,' said Margaret. 'If you're insistent on taking the blame, there's still a very strong case for self-defence. I'd say you have three rather reputable witnesses who'll speak in your favour.'

'Reputable?' laughed Carol. 'Is that the word for it?'

Catherine was right, of course. She had killed Jim. Sometimes, when she'd first come back to prison, Carol had wondered if she'd done the right thing. She'd fought so hard to clear her name, to stop herself ending up back here, and then she'd given it all up by taking the blame for a murder she hadn't committed. Now, she knew she'd done the right thing.

The four sat in the moment, enjoying each other's company.

'Are you sure you want me on the outside again? I do get itchy. I'll probably kill one of you eventually.'

And then, after Carol Quinn, one of Britain's most notorious serial killers, had told her best friends that she'd most likely kill one of them one day, they laughed and talked about a new recipe

Margaret had just seen for lemon meringue pie. Apparently, the secret was to use sour cream, which they all agreed was the most shocking thing they'd heard in years.

ACKNOWLEDGEMENTS

I find acknowledgements a little embarrassing as it has always felt, to me, like writing an acceptance speech for an award I haven't won. However, it would be rude of me not to acknowledge the part that Ed Wood, whilst he was still Publishing Director at Sphere Books, played in devising the premise to this book. He also helped me to push my middling IQ to its limits and conjure up what I hope was a satisfying murder mystery.

Since I am now here, writing an acknowledgements, I should take the time to thank some other people. Thank you to everyone at Sphere Books and Little, Brown and Company for all the work they have put into this book. I take full responsibility for any typos that remain. Particular thanks go to Jack Butler and Frances Rooney for expertly shepherding this thing to completion.

Thank you to everyone at Berkley Books, most especially Michelle Vega, for taking a chance on a Brit and for helping, I hope, to make my most English sentences palatable to an American audience.

Huge thanks to Gordon Wise, my agent, for frequently settling my nerves.

Thanks to my mum for passing on her love of books and to my dad for passing on his habit of analysing absolutely everything. Perhaps it's a trait that can be annoying in real life, but it certainly comes in handy as a writer.

Finally, thank you to Laurie for supporting and tolerating me in every way possible and to Louis for being the kindest and funniest kid I have ever met. I'd like to take this moment to congratulate Louis on recently reaching stage three in his swimming lessons. He worked very hard to get there and deserves every bit of praise he gets.